Roundup
- of the -
Street Rovers

Trailblazer Books

*Hero Tales: A Family Treasury of True Stories
From the Lives of Christian Heroes* (Volumes I, II, III, & IV)

*Curriculum guide available.
Written by Julia Pferdehirt with Dave & Neta Jackson.

Roundup
– of the –
Street Rovers

Dave & Neta Jackson

Illustrated by Anne Gavitt

BETHANY HOUSE PUBLISHERS
MINNEAPOLIS, MINNESOTA 55438

Published by Bethany House Publishers
A Ministry of Bethany Fellowship International
11400 Hampshire Avenue South
Bloomington, Minnesota 55438
www.bethanyhouse.com

Printed in the United States of America by
Bethany Press International, Bloomington, Minnesota 55438

Library of Congress Cataloging-in-Publication Data

Jackson, Dave.
    Roundup of the street rovers : Charles Loring Brace / by Dave & Neta Jackson ; text illustrations by Anne Gavitt.
       p. cm. — (Trailblazer books)
    Summary: In 1854, a group of children who come from different circumstances to the Children's Aid Society in New York come under the care of Rev. Charles Brace, who eventually finds homes for them in Dowagiac, Michigan.
       ISBN 0–7642–2269–4 (pbk.)
    1. Brace, Charles Loring, 1826–1890—Juvenile fiction. [1. Brace, Charles Loring, 1826–1890—Fiction. 2. Children's Aid Society (New York, N.Y.)—Fiction. 3. Orphans—Fiction. 4. Orphan trains—Fiction. 5. Christian life—Fiction.] I. Jackson, Neta. II. Gavitt, Anne, ill. III. Title.
PZ7.J132418 Ro 2001
[Fic]   dc21
                                               2001002773

The first three chapters introduce three sets of children, showing the different types of heartbreaking situations that thrust children onto the Children's Aid Society of New York. All the situations are based on true stories that happened to real children (though the names and details of the situations have been changed) during the history of the Children's Aid Society, but are merged here into 1854 in a fictionalized way to create this book. The activities and humanitarian efforts of Charles Loring Brace are all authentic.

The first "orphan train" to leave New York for the West in September 1854 used "emigrant cars"—boxcars—to transport the orphans from the Children's Aid Society. But Rev. Brace insisted that all future orphans would ride in regular passenger cars—therefore we placed the children in this book in regular passenger cars to convey the usual experience of the orphan train riders.

The first orphan train west arrived in Dowagiac, Michigan, early Sunday morning, September 24, 1854, with forty-six children. All were placed by the end of the week. What happened after that in this book is fictional.

Find us on the Web at . . .

TrailblazerBooks.com

- Meet the authors.

- Read the first chapter of each book—with the pictures.

- Track the Trailblazers around the world on a map.

- Use the historical timeline to find out what other important events were happening in the world at the time of each Trailblazer story.

- Discover how the authors research their books and link to some of the same sources they used where you can learn more about these heroes.

- Write to the authors.

- Explore frequently asked questions about writing and Trailblazer books.

Just point your browser to *www.trailblazerbooks.com*

CONTENTS

DAVE AND NETA JACKSON are a full-time husband/wife writing team who have authored and coauthored many books on marriage and family, the church, relationships, and other subjects. Their books for children include the TRAILBLAZER series and *Hero Tales,* volumes I, II, III, and IV. The Jacksons make their home in Evanston, Illinois.

Chapter 1

Street Tough

B ack it up, boys! Back it up . . . whoa!"
The belly-deep voice from outside in the alley woke up Kip O'Reilly. Down in the dark cellar of the brick tenement building, the thirteen-year-old boy braced himself for the next sound: hard chunks of coal thundering down the metal chute into the coal bin.

Uhh. Coal wagon. Saturday morning. Time to get moving.

Kip pushed away the sleeping boy sprawled next to him and sat up on the lumpy mattress. Gradually his eyes adjusted to the thin gray light seeping through the coal-dust-covered windows. Outside, he heard the *clop,*

9

clop, clop of the coal-wagon horse heading back down the alley.

"Wake up, Billy!" he ordered, giving the body next to him a shove. "Coal wagon's come an' gone. Git out there and pick up them pieces."

Billy groaned, but stumbled to his feet. Both boys were already "dressed," having slept in their clothes. Kip boosted the other scrawny boy, all knees and elbows, through the narrow window that Kip's gang used to come and go into the cellar, then took to waking the other three boys huddled together on the thin mattress. "C'mon, Ned . . . shake those bones, Hooter . . . git up, Smack. What makes you rovers think you can sit round all day like a bunch o' swells?" With little ceremony, he passed out hunks of bread left over from the weekend's pickings for breakfast.

Nine-year-old Billy wriggled back through the window and dropped to the stone floor, his pockets bulging with hunks of coal that had fallen off the coal wagon. Kip thumped him on the head. "A sack! A sack! Ya s'posed to use a 'tater sack. Now look at ya. How ya gonna shine shoes lookin' like that? Get out o' them pants. . . . Smack, you and Billy take that bundle o' dirty clothes up to Mrs. Conner when it gets full daylight, see if she'll wash 'em fer us. Take the coal Billy picked up—that oughter be payment enough."

Kip, the oldest of the lot, continued to give orders for the day. Billy and Smack would scavenge the dump bins behind the greengrocers for food. Ned and Hooter would take the shoeshine boxes and head uptown where the "swells" did business. Kip would pick up his papers at the *New York Times* drop and work his corner. "Anybody with time left over, head for the docks." The fishmongers often let the street boys do odd jobs in exchange for fresh fish. "Meet back here at five o'clock, see what we got."

"But I'm hungry now," Billy sulked. His pinched face was testimony to too many missed meals.

"No thievin'!" Kip growled. Not that Kip had any scruples about taking what they needed to survive on the streets of New York. But the younger boys were clumsy and often got caught by the storekeeper or the local policeman. Then he had to use their hard-earned pocket change getting one of the gang out of the slammer. Better if they stuck together, pooled their money, and let him take the risks.

A rosy dawn was washing the crowded tenement buildings in the Five Points district with a false cheerfulness as Kip trotted quickly past the rotting garbage in the gutters. Five cobblestone streets converged at angles, giving the rat-infested slum its notorious name. He dodged horse-drawn cabs, milk wagons, rag pickers, and scrap-metal scavengers getting an early start on the day. A lone drunk tottered down the street ahead of him, and Kip slowed. An old memory tugged at him. Could it be—? Nah. His old man would've drunk himself to death by this time. And who cared if he had? Not Kip. His da had sold him off four years back to a shoe tanner to get money for his drink. *"Gotta learn a trade,"* the old man had said. But Kip had been only eight, and all he did in the tannery was haul buckets of coal and water, blow the fire, and sweep up the leather shavings twelve hours a day.

Nah, Kip had had enough of being "indentured" as a servant. "Do this . . . do that"—always the worst work with no pay! So he'd run away and made a life for himself on the streets. *Not a bad life, either,* he thought as he slyly lifted a handful of crackers from a barrel outside a greengrocer and took off running down a side street.

He arrived at the newspaper drop-off—just a wooden stall set up on the corner of Walker and Centre Streets—just as the *New York Times* wagon was pulling up with its load of morning papers. "Mornin', Mr. Tibbs!" he called out cheerily to the driver, grabbing the bridle of the sturdy bay horse and giving the animal a friendly pat.

"Hmpf." The driver acknowledged Kip with a grunt, opened the back door of the enclosed wagon, and started hauling bundles of papers into the wooden stall. Soon newsboys from all over the Five Points district would show up to get their papers and head out to different street corners. Each boy got a penny for every paper he sold. Kip usually sold his whole bundle of twenty-five papers. Twenty-five papers, twenty-five cents.

But right now his eye was on the feed bag of corn hanging on the side of the wagon. The sturdy brown horse stood in its traces breathing hard from its fast trot through the cobblestone streets. It wouldn't miss just one handful of corn. . . .

Kip sidled along the far side of the wagon, stood on a spoke of the front wheel, and reached deep into the feed bag. With a quick movement he stuffed a handful of corn into his pocket, then pursed his lips in a casual whistle as he came around to pick up his papers.

"How many o' them papers you takin' today?" The drop-off driver took out a note pad and squinted at Kip.

"Twenty-five to start." Kip filled up a sturdy canvas bag with newspapers as the man wrote down the number. "Say, what's the headlines today?"

Tibbs spit on the street and glanced at a paper. "Uh—'British Troops Die in Crimea'... an' 'Runaway Slave Kidnapped in Boston.' Huh. You'd think nothin' ever happens in New York."

Kip just waved and set off for the corner of Canal and Centre—*his* corner—where he knew Pogo would be waiting for him.

Sure enough, as he dropped his bundle of papers on the curb just outside Smith & Sons Haberdashery, a gray-and-white pigeon fluttered to a landing, just inches from the toes of Kip's badly scuffed shoes. Cocking its red eye, the pigeon strutted back and forth, a demanding *cuck-coo, cuck-coo* in its throat.

"Hey there, Pogo." A grin spread over Kip's face, and his blue eyes danced beneath the shock of nearly black hair. Could hardly tell it was the same pigeon he'd found a year ago with a broken wing. "What makes ya think I got somethin' for ya, eh?" He turned his back on the pigeon, pulled out an armload of

papers, and started hawking headlines. "Brits Die in the Crimey! Runaway Slave Kidnapped! Git yer *Times* here!"

The pigeon began hopping up and down, beating its wings.

Kip turned around. "What ya so mad fer? I'm just teasin' ya. Here ..." The boy dug into his pants pocket and drew out the fistful of corn. The pigeon flew onto his coat sleeve and began pecking the corn right out of his hand.

As the pigeon ate, Kip continued to hail passers-by. "Git yer *New York Times* right here! Only a nickel!—Thanks, lady ... Read about the Crimey War! Right here ... only a nickel! ... Top o' the mornin' to ya, sir ... Git yer *Times*!" The pigeon held on tight to Kip's coat sleeve as he made his transactions.

Kip had almost sold his first bundle of papers when a tall gentleman stopped. "Good morning, Kip." The man was still in his twenties and sturdily built, but properly outfitted in long coat, trousers, and derby hat. "Not sure who's selling more papers this morning—you or that pigeon of yours." The man's smile was warm and friendly. "Still got a paper for me?"

"Yes, sir, Rev ... uh, Rev. Brace, sir." Kip gave the man his next to last paper and pocketed the nickel. But the man did not hurry on.

"Say, Kip. We're having some Boys' Meetings over at the Children's Aid Society. I'd like you to come tomorrow night."

Kip looked at the man warily. "Uh, don' think I can, Rev. Wouldn't want ter leave my boys—they kinder depend on me, ya know."

"*Bring* the boys! The more the merrier! What do you say?"

Kip looked up and down the street, hoping a potential customer was close by to get him off the spot. But the sidewalk was momentarily deserted. He narrowed his eyes and looked back at the friendly face. "Boys' Meetin', huh? That just another name fer Sunday school?"

Rev. Charles Brace threw back his head and laughed. Gray eyes twinkled under prominent brows. "Now, come on, Kip. I'm a regular customer of yours. Always come to this corner to buy my paper. The Society would like to help some of the street rovers. It's a hard life, and you know it. They're suspicious, just like you. But a lot of the boys look up to you. You're a leader. If *you* came to the Boys' Meeting, they would, too, and that's the all of it." Grinning again through his neatly trimmed beard and mustache, the man held out his hand. "So, will you come? Let's shake on it, man to man."

❖ ❖ ❖ ❖

"You *shook* on it?" Hooter said, his eyes popping. "What you go doin' that fer!"

"Yeah. We was wantin' to play some numbers tomorrow—maybe get us a policy ticket or two." Smack stuck his lip out, mirroring the faces of Billy and Ned.

"You can do that any ol' time. *Tomorrow night* we're goin' on over to the Aid Society. They got them

16

a Boys' Meeting an' want us to come." Kip tried to look more confident than he felt. "Come on. You know the Rev. He's a good 'un."

"Yeah. I seed him up visitin' the Conners, the lady what does our wash," Smack admitted. "That Mrs. Conners, she don't look so good. But she took the clothes, said she was grateful for the coal."

"Awright, then. Agreed?"

Reluctantly, the little gang of boys nodded. And true to their word, the next evening they swaggered through the dusky streets, acting like they were going to a fair. Broadway wasn't far, but by the time they arrived at the Children's Aid Society, they'd picked up half a dozen more street rovers looking for anything to pass the time.

They arrived noisily to a room already half full of boys of all ages. Kip noticed a rover with red hair who'd once tried to take his corner, but Kip had bloodied his nose and the kid had held a grudge ever since. Kip almost backed out, but just then Rev. Brace slapped him heartily on the back. "Knew I could count on you, Kip. Welcome, welcome, boys. Off with your caps, now . . . just sit down. We'll be starting soon."

There was a mad scramble for the benches. One of the other street rovers pushed Billy off the bench he'd claimed, and Billy took it personally. In half a second, the two boys were on the floor, punching each other with abandon. In the other half second, the rest of the room erupted, yelling encouragement to "their boy."

Rev. Brace and another gentleman pulled the boys off each other and restored a calm of sorts. "Mr. Tracey," boomed Rev. Brace, a firm hand on the shoulders of the two fighters, "let's get some gospel songs under their belts."

The man had a good tenor voice and launched into "Soldiers of Christ, Arise." He sang by himself for the first few lines, but the words and tune were so compelling that soon many of the boys heartily joined in, though half a step behind since they didn't know the words. " '. . . wrestle, and fight, and pray; Tread all the powers of darkness down. . . .' "

Then Mr. Tracey opened his big black Bible. "How many of you boys know the story of the Pharisee and the publican?"

Not a hand raised.

"Well, then." Mr. Tracey cast an anxious eye at Rev. Brace. "Who knows what a 'publican' is?"

Kip shot up his hand. "An alderman, sire! What keeps a pothouse."

Hearty laughter from the boys.

Mr. Tracey's face reddened. "Alderman! P-pothouse! Wha—?"

Kip glared. What was wrong with what he said? Didn't the man say "publican"? Had to have *some-*thing to do with a pub or pothouse. Then he saw that the Rev was trying to stifle a smile behind his hand. Kip grinned. The Rev was all right.

Just then, the redheaded street rover snarled in Kip's ear, "Think ya smart, don'cha, ya little Mick."

"Who ya callin' a Mick?" Kip gave the boy a good

elbow to the stomach.

In a flash the boy was on top of Kip, tumbling over the benches, and once again the room erupted into a brawl.

Another peace-keeping mission by Brace and Tracey restored the room to order, and Rev. Brace talked to the boys about the Lodging House they were starting for newsboys and other street rovers. Then Rev. Brace brought the Boys' Meeting to a snappy close. "See you next week, boys. Glad you came, Kip. Good to see you, Hooter." He shook hands with nearly all the boys as they filed out. Then Kip heard him say as the door closed, "Well. Pretty good start, wouldn't you say, Tracey?"

✧ ✧ ✧ ✧

The next morning Kip was back on his corner, hawking the day's newspaper, Pogo riding shotgun on his shoulder. "Git yer Monday *Times* right here! One nickel!" Kip grinned at his customers.

"What a pleasant young man," murmured an old woman to the policeman who was idly walking his beat. But Kip wasn't thinking about his customers. He was thinking about the Boys' Meeting the night before at the Children's Aid Society. He chuckled to himself. The Rev got a little more than he bargained for!

Pogo walked along the back of Kip's shabby jacket and took up a beady-eyed watch on his other shoulder.

"Look, Lauren! Look at the pet pigeon!"

19

"Lena—wait!"

A little girl about eight ran up to Kip. Behind her, a stylish woman in brown wearing a poke bonnet with velvet trim held the hand of a slightly older girl. The two girls wore matching tight-waisted coats and had shoulder-length honey-colored hair. Sisters, probably.

"Nasty pigeon," sniffed the lady in brown. "Don't step in its droppings, girls. Ugh."

Kip ignored the remark. A customer was a customer. "Paper, lady?"

"I suppose—if you're sure it doesn't have any bird droppings on it."

"Oh no, ma'am." Kip almost wished it did, just to see the lady get upset.

"Can your pigeon do tricks?" The smaller girl cocked her head, imitating the pigeon.

"Sure, missy." Kip was just about to dig out the last bit of corn from his pocket to show how Pogo ate out of his hand, when out of the corner of his eye he saw a familiar face coming his way—fat, red, and scowling. Kip tried to duck his head. Too late. The greengrocer who "supplied" Kip's daily breakfast caught his eye.

"You . . . there you are, you little thief! Police! Police! Catch that boy."

Pogo flapped his wings and darted into the air as Kip dropped his bag of papers at the feet of the two girls and ran.

Chapter 2

Poor Little Rich Girls

Lauren Rogers grabbed her little sister by the coat sleeve and pulled her back as the newsboy rudely dumped his papers on the sidewalk and took off running. A short, round man in shirt sleeves and a not very clean apron ran after the boy, yelling, "Stop, thief! Stop that boy!"

"What's happening, Lauren?" wailed Lena.

The beat policeman, hearing the commotion, took up the chase. Lauren didn't know what the boy had done, but she found herself hoping he would get away. The policeman snagged the boy by the back of his coat just as he tried to dart into an alley. The fat man ran up, waving his arms and pointing accusing fingers at the newsboy.

"Well, I *never*!" The lady in brown snatched the hands of both Lauren and Lena and started walking briskly back the way they had come.

"But—but what's going to happen to the boy's pigeon?" Lena's whine grated on Lauren's nerves.

Miss Wilson yanked on Lena's hand. "Shush now! Don't ask such foolish things. Proper little girls don't raise their voices in public."

"But—"

"Shush, I said! Humph. Pigeon, indeed."

Lauren sighed. Their governess seemed to be cross quite often lately. The older girl looked back over her shoulder, hoping to get a glimpse of the newsboy. But the policeman, the boy, and the fat man in the apron had all disappeared.

The trio turned off Canal Street, and Miss Wilson's neat, buttoned shoes under the hem of the brown wool coat went *tap, tap, tap, tap* as they walked past the brownstone homes until the middle of the block, where they turned up a short flight of steps. She unlocked the door with its leaded glass panel and paused by a small table in the foyer. Lauren watched anxiously as the governess flipped through a small stack of mail sitting on the table.

"Nothing!" Miss Wilson threw down the letters and hustled the girls up a flight of stairs to her second-floor apartment.

Nothing—again. Lauren knew that Miss Wilson eagerly awaited the mail each day, hoping to get a letter from Lauren and Lena's parents. But Lauren had lost track of how long it had been since her mother and father had written.

The last letter had been a short note explaining that Mr. Rogers' business in Europe was not finished, so could Miss Wilson care for the girls one more month? A bank draft was enclosed for the girls' expenses and another month's pay for the governess.

But that month went by, then another, and another. No parents. No letters. No more money.

As Miss Wilson and the girls entered the apartment, Lena snatched up a rather worn stuffed rabbit lying on the floor of the entryway. "Muffin! You waited for me!" The girl hugged the soft toy.

"Lena, put that thing down and take off your coat," snapped Miss Wilson. She was still a fairly young woman, in her late twenties, and rather pretty except for the frown that had taken up residence between her eyes. "Eight years old is too old for such a baby toy."

Lena's frown matched the governess's. "Muffin is *not* a baby toy. He's my *friend*." The little girl stomped off down the long hall.

Miss Wilson sighed as she took off her feathered hat. Lauren silently hung up her coat and followed Lena. In the bedroom the girls shared in Miss Wilson's apartment, Lena sat pouting on the bed, holding Muffin in a stranglehold. Her little sister probably needed a hug, but Lauren's own tears lurked dangerously near the surface. Instead, she plopped down on the window seat and looked up at the slice of sky she could see above the brownstone next door.

She wondered what happened to the newsboy who got caught by the policeman. Did he have parents who were worried about *him*?

Lauren was tired of staying with Miss Wilson. She wanted to go home. Why did their mother always have to travel with their father? Why had she stopped writing? Didn't she care about them anymore? Lauren tried to picture her mother and father, but the image of their faces was fuzzy in her mind. A lump of fear pushed hot tears down her cheeks. Maybe their parents had forgotten all about them and they'd have to stay with Miss Wilson *forever*.

Lauren kept expecting Miss Wilson to come in and begin their school lessons, but the governess did not appear. They always started their school lessons after their morning walk to get the newspaper and pick up any groceries needed for that day. But today they'd come back early without any groceries. And now Miss Wilson wasn't starting their lessons.

Why wasn't anything like it was supposed to be?

Down the hall Lauren heard the bell by the apartment door jangle. Someone was downstairs at the front door. She looked over at the bed. Lena had fallen asleep, still clutching Muffin. Brushing the wetness off her cheeks, Lauren tiptoed over to the bedroom door and slowly cracked it open. She heard footsteps, the apartment door opening and closing, and the murmur of voices.

Who was it? Probably Miss Wilson's beau. He'd been around a lot lately. He was all right, she guessed, except he was usually annoyed because

Miss Wilson always had to take the girls with her when he came courting.

Lauren opened the door wider and peered down the dimly lit hallway. The voices were coming from the front room. She crept silently down the hall until she could make out what the voices were saying.

"But what about our wedding day? We set the date three months ago!"

"I know, I know, Johnny! I thought the Rogerses would be back long before now, plenty of time to give my notice. But now—oh, I don't know what to do."

Lauren could hear Miss Wilson pacing back and forth in the front room.

"How long has it been since they sent you money to take care of the girls—or paid *you*, for that matter?"

"Oh . . . six, seven weeks. Almost two months."

"Two months! That's grounds for neglect!"

"Shh, Johnny! The girls will hear you."

The two voices in the front room lowered, and Lauren couldn't hear what they were saying anymore. She tiptoed back to the bedroom and lay down beside Lena. Neglect? What did that mean? And what if their parents hadn't come back by the time Miss Wilson got married? What would happen to them then?

Lauren couldn't stop the tears now. Her shoulders shook and she cried silently until she fell asleep beside Lena.

✧ ✧ ✧

"Come on, girls. Finish your lunch. Then we're going for a ride. Wouldn't you like that?"

A ride? Lauren looked up from her plate of bread and cold chicken from last night's dinner. They hadn't taken a ride in a carriage since the letters and money stopped coming.

"But we haven't done our lessons yet!" Lena was still pouting and determined to be contrary.

Miss Wilson smiled stiffly. "We're taking a vacation today. No lessons. . . . Come on, now, quick, quick."

The girls finished their lunch and shrugged into their coats. Lena tucked Muffin into the crook of her arm.

"Not the rabbit," scolded Miss Wilson, jerking the stuffed animal out of Lena's arm and tossing it on a chair. "If you must *insist* on keeping that shabby toy, at least don't drag it out in public."

"But I want—!"

Miss Wilson hustled the wailing Lena down the stairs and out the front door. A cab was waiting.

"Take us to 683 Broadway," Miss Wilson told the driver before she climbed into the carriage after the girls.

As the horse trotted down their street and turned into the traffic, Lauren tried to read Miss Wilson's face. Where were they going? Not just for a ride. She'd given the driver an address.

The cab passed the corner where the newsboy had been selling his papers. Lauren saw a lone pigeon walking back and forth, pecking now and then at a speck on the sidewalk.

The cab turned down one street, then another, until it finally pulled up beside a plain building with the sign *New York Children's Aid Society*. Miss Wilson told the driver to wait, and briskly herded the girls through the front door.

A tall man with a neatly trimmed dark beard rose from his desk and greeted them. "May I help you, ladies? My name is Rev. Charles Brace. And you are . . . ?"

Miss Wilson spoke quickly, as though speaking lines from a play that she was afraid she'd forget. "These children"—she pushed Lauren and Lena forward—"their parents have abandoned them. I can no longer care for them. I . . . I am getting married, you see, and going away."

Lauren stared in shock as Miss Wilson briefly filled in the reverend on the last whereabouts of Mr. and Mrs. Rogers, and handed him the last letter that had arrived from overseas. Miss Wilson was just going to leave them here with this—this total stranger!

The governess could not look the girls in the eyes. "I'm sorry, girls. These people will look after you until your parents return. I'm . . . I'm sure it will be soon." With that, Miss Wilson turned and swept quickly out the door.

Anger sent Lauren running after her. "What about our things? Our clothes and books and . . . and . . ."

"I'll send them over tonight, or tomorrow. Goodbye." Miss Wilson stepped into the cab, and the horse pulled away.

In the doorway, Lauren and Lena watched the cab turn a corner and disappear, their mouths hanging open. Lauren felt a large, gentle hand on her shoulder.

"Come on in now, girls. You've had a bad shock.

Come, come, sit and tell me your story. Mrs. Delaney! Can you bring these girls some tea and milk?"

Rev. Brace listened as Lauren told their story between fits of angry tears. Lena just sat there, her face a stoic mask. Mrs. Delaney, the "matron" in charge of the girls, arrived with a tray of tea and cookies. Both Lauren and Lena shook their heads. They weren't hungry.

"This is a very perplexing situation," said the kindly man. "I promise you, Lauren and Lena, that I will do everything I can to find your parents. In the meantime, Mrs. Delaney will try to make you comfortable upstairs in our girls' dormitory—we have a few other homeless girls who are staying with us at present."

He stood up. "I'm going out, Mrs. Delaney," he said to the rosy-cheeked woman who looked rather like an apple dumpling to Lauren. "I still haven't got my newspaper. Young master Kip wasn't at the corner this morning when I got there . . . just his pigeon looking a bit worried, if I do say so myself."

Lauren's eyes widened. "A pigeon, sir? The newsboy with the pigeon? We saw him this morning." She told Rev. Brace about the man who yelled "Stop, thief!" and the policeman who'd given chase.

"Hmm. Looks like Kip O'Reilly's free-living ways have caught up with him," murmured Rev. Brace. "Thank you, Lauren. Now, go with Mrs. Delaney. She'll show you your beds and give you some supper. I'll see you again at our night school at the church."

Night school? Lauren felt dizzy. Everything was

happening so fast. She held tightly to Lena's hand and followed Mrs. Delaney up some narrow stairs to a plain, square room that held six beds. It was nothing like their large bedroom at home or even at Miss Wilson's, full of books and toys and thick comforters. Since they had no suitcases to unpack, the girls just laid their coats on two of the beds and meekly followed the plump woman down the stairs again.

Mrs. Delaney bustled around the kitchen, where a pot of stew bubbled on the iron cookstove. Finally Lauren worked up the courage to ask what a night school was. "Oh, just another one o' Rev. Brace's big ideas." Mrs. Delaney chuckled. "But it's a good 'un, his night school. For the street rovers and others who can't—or don't—go to reg'lar school. A lot of 'em work young, helpin' out their families, and some just don't have the money for proper clothes or books. The ones who stay here have to pay for bed and food, so they've got to work, they do. All in all, the night school helps the bunch of 'em get their education."

Lauren felt the blood drain out of her face. *The ones who stay here have to pay for bed and food.* "But . . . but we don't have any money to—to pay. . . ."

"Now, don't you worry. I'm sure Rev. Brace will work something out. He's never turned a child away yet. Come on, now, set these plates out. I hear the other girls coming in for supper."

Lauren and Lena watched like frightened rabbits as three other girls came into the kitchen, laughing and talking. They were older—maybe fourteen or fifteen—and they walked with the tilted chins and big strides of girls who knew their way around. They looked quizzically at the sisters, but after a brief "howdy-do," they basically ignored the newcomers. Lauren bent her head over her bowl of stew, looking up only to make sure Lena was eating something. From the conversation around the table, she decided the girls must work as servants at some of the finer houses. When her parents were home, Lauren had seen such girls scrubbing pots or ironing sheets at her own house and had never given them much thought.

Her lip trembled. Would she and Lena end up as servants, too?

After supper, Mrs. Delaney asked the older girls to take Lauren and Lena with them to the night school. Obediently, the two sisters got their coats and followed the older girls down the street and around the corner to a modest brown brick church. They went down some side steps into a large basement room, where Rev. Brace and several other adults were sorting about twenty girls of different ages into "classes." Relief eased the tension in Lauren's stomach to see several of the women dressed like Miss Wilson and her mother—dark-colored taffeta dresses trimmed in lace over a modest hoop, all in the current fashion. Here were people from *her* world.

Rev. Brace caught sight of them and headed their way, bringing a girl a couple years older than Lauren with him. "Peggy," he said to the girl, "Lauren and Lena will be with us for a while. Could you take them under your wing tonight till they get adjusted?"

The girl shrugged. "Sure. Come on. Ya can sit in my class till they figger where to put ya. Say, what's wrong with the little 'un?"

Big tears sat like puddles in Lena's eyes. Suddenly she opened her mouth and let out a wail. "I . . . I . . . I want M-M-Muffin!"

Lauren tried to shush her little sister. Everyone was looking at them. But a dark realization hung unspoken between them: Miss Wilson had never returned with their clothes or belongings. All they had in the world were the clothes on their backs and each other.

Chapter 3

Tenement Tragedy

Peggy Conner waited impatiently while the new girl wiped her little sister's nose and tried to comfort her. What were a couple of "swells" doing at the Children's Aid Society, anyway? Their wool coats had velvet collars, and frilly pantalettes peeked out beneath their dresses. Probably thought they were too good to be here with a bunch of Irish immigrants.

And who was "Muffin," anyway?

Still, Rev. Brace had asked her to look out for them. She'd do it for Rev. Brace. After all, he was the one who had convinced her stepfather to let her and Carlotta come to the night school. Mike

Conner hadn't wanted to let the girls go. *"Need the girls ta help their mother with the washin' she takes in. My wife ain't well, cain't ya see that, Reverend? Coughin' all the time. An' I cain't get home from the docks till seven."*

Rev. Brace had nodded. *"I know the girls are a big help, Mr. Conner. That's why we have the school in the evening, for families just like yours. Think of their future, man!"*

Mrs. Conner had sided with Rev. Brace. *"Don't want my children livin' and dyin' in this rathole, Mike. They need schoolin'."*

Finally Mike Conner had relented, and Peggy worked even harder to help Ma get all the washing and delivering done each day before time to leave for school at five o'clock.

This evening Peggy had felt a little uneasy when it was time to leave. Ma had been coughing something awful all day, and six-year-old Davey could be a handful cooped up in their tiny tenement apartment. But Ma had insisted that the girls go. Peggy was glad, because they were reading *Gulliver's Travels* at school, and she didn't want to miss the next part.

She stuck out her hand to the new girl. "Name's Peggy. I'm twelve. How old are ya . . . Lauren, is it?"

Lauren nodded. "I'm ten. This is Lena. She's eight."

Considering how fancy their clothes were, both girls looked pale and sad.

"Eight? She could be in my sister Carlotta's

class . . . but never mind. She can stay with you. It don't matter the first time."

Peggy led the new girls over to a corner of the room where other girls about her age were clacking away with pairs of knitting needles. Long rectangles of knitted yarn hung from the needles. The teacher, a young woman with a gentle voice, was reading aloud from *Gulliver's Travels* as the girls worked.

"Wool scarves," whispered Peggy. "We make 'em for the Society to give out to the street rovers when the cold's bad. You knit?"

Lauren shook her head.

"Well, here, I'll show ya." Peggy got a pair of needles and a ball of green yarn, cast on forty stitches, and knitted a row or two, showing Lauren how to loop the yarn over the right needle and pull it through. Then she picked up her own knitting, hoping the new girl was a fast learner so she could listen to the story of Gulliver.

But it was hopeless. Lauren kept asking for help, and even then her knitting turned into a tangled mess. When the lesson changed to melting tallow and pouring candles, Lauren was clumsy and burned her hand. And the little one—Lena—wouldn't even try. She just sat next to her sister looking like she was going to cry.

But when it was time to write and do numbers, Peggy noticed that Lauren was done before anyone else—and her work was neat, too. Even so, Peggy was relieved when Rev. Brace rang the bell that night school was over. She hoped she didn't have to baby-sit these two swells *every* night, or she'd never learn anything herself.

Peggy put on her homespun hooded cape, then tied Carlotta's hood around her chin as the two Rogers girls buttoned their store-bought coats. "Are you coming back to the Society with us?" Lauren asked hopefully.

"Nah. Carlotta and me—we're not orphans, ya know. Street rovers, neither." Peggy started to toss her head proudly but saw Lauren wince at the word *orphans*. "Anyway, our step-da unloads ships down at the docks, picks us up when it's dark. He's probably outside right now, cussin' 'cause we're late."

But Mike Conner was not waiting as the girls spilled out of the church basement and took off in half a dozen different directions. Carriages were waiting to take the volunteer teachers home to their families in better wards of the city. Mrs. Delaney was waiting to shepherd the two new girls back to the Children's Aid Society. Rev. Brace locked the side door of the church, then seemed surprised to see Peggy and Carlotta still waiting on the narrow brick sidewalk. "Your father not here yet?"

Peggy shook her head. A small frown puckered her eyebrows. Had something happened to Ma? Or Davey? She shook off the worry. More likely their stepfather had stopped off for a drink and lost track of time. Wouldn't be the first time.

"That's all right. I'll walk you home." Rev. Brace smiled and took each of the girls by the hand. "Been wanting to stop by to see your mother anyway."

The May evening shadows lengthened and dark-ened as the trio walked silently through the streets of the Five Points district. Peggy didn't feel like talking. She just wanted to get home quickly. Tall tenement buildings towered all around them. Her feet picked up the pace as they crossed the five-way intersection of Park Street, Baxter, and Worth, which gave the slum its name. It was hard to avoid the garbage on the narrow sidewalks in the dark, but walking in the streets, full of horse manure that rarely got cleaned up, was just as chancy.

As the girls and Brace turned up Mulberry, a set of young street rovers filled the sidewalk, tossing cards and yelling bids in the pool of light from a broken window nearby. But seeing the girls and Rev. Brace, they all jumped up and fell silent, staring.

"Hello, Billy. Hello, Hooter," said Rev. Brace. He looked at each face in the dim light. "You boys know where Kip is?"

"Dunno, Rev. Ain't seed 'im since this mornin'. We been worried." Billy snatched his cap off and glanced awkwardly at Peggy and Carlotta. "Uh, sorry 'bout your ma."

Peggy stiffened. "What about my ma?"

The boys looked uneasily at each other, then faded into the shadows.

Rushing ahead of Rev. Brace and Carlotta, Peggy dashed up the wooden outside stairs in back of their tenement building. On the third-floor landing, she pushed open the door of the Conner apartment and called out, "Ma? Ma!"

A light flickered in the room, but there was no answer. Rev. Brace and Carlotta came in behind her. Peggy pushed aside heavy, damp sheets hanging every which way in the Conner kitchen and saw her stepfather sitting motionless at the table, his hands around a dark bottle. On a cot in the corner, six-year-old Davey lay asleep, all tucked up like a newborn baby. A lard-oil lamp flickered in the middle of the table, pushing sooty smoke into the dank air.

"Mr. Conner?" Rev. Brace walked over and laid a hand on the man's shoulders. "What's happened here? Where's your wife?"

Fear stuck in Peggy's throat as her stepfather looked up slowly, his eyes hollow, his mouth drooping. "Dead," he mumbled, lowering his eyes and just staring at the bottle again. "Found 'er dead on the floor when I comes home from work . . . the boy wailing, tryin' to wake 'er up." His big Adam's apple rose and fell as he tried to swallow, as if words were stuck in his throat. "They took 'er 'way already."

The big Irish dock worker looked up at Rev. Brace once more, not seeming to see the girls, who were crying now. "What am I goin' ta do now, Reverend, eh? I cain't take care o' three little 'uns workin' at the dock all day. They was her kids 'fore I even married her, when their father died. Tell me, Reverend— what am I s'posed ta do?"

Shakily, Peggy made her feet walk forward. "I . . . I'll help, Da. Carlotta, too. We'll do the washin' . . . and take care o' Davey while you're at work. I can cook, too."

Mike Conner just stared dully at his oldest stepdaughter, then turned his stare back to his hands and the brown bottle.

Rev. Brace laid a comforting hand on Peggy's shoulder and drew her aside. "I'll try to find out where the undertaker has taken your mother and arrange for a burial service. I'm sorry, child. This is a large burden at your age. Come to school tomorrow night if you can—bring Davey, too. That's all right. But if you can't, I'll come again. I promise."

Peggy and Carlotta cried themselves to sleep that night, curled together in a narrow, sagging bed behind a curtain. The glow from the lamp on the table where their stepfather just sat, unmoving, silent, cast flickering shadows from the other side of the curtain till sleep swallowed up their grief.

❖ ❖ ❖ ❖

The lamp was out and the thin light of morning filled the tenement apartment when Peggy awoke to Davey shaking her shoulder. "I'm hungry, Peggy. Wake up. I'm hungry."

With a start, Peggy untangled herself from Carlotta's embrace. She had meant to get up before dawn and make breakfast for Da before he left for work. Was he still asleep?

A quick glance around the apartment told her that Mike Conner was already gone. Peggy felt like kicking herself. Hadn't she promised her stepfather she would help? Now he'd be angry and feel like she was just going to be a burden.

Well, she'd show him different. She was big and strong for twelve. She'd already helped Ma with the washing. She hadn't done much cooking, but how hard could that be?

Peggy woke up Carlotta and set her to dressing Davey while she threw precious hunks of coal into the cookstove and fanned the embers till the coal caught and smoldered. A huge ache clutched at her insides as she grabbed her mother's shawl and the water bucket, but she clenched her teeth and clattered down the outside steps to the small courtyard between their tenement building and the next. She stood in line to use one of the smelly privies before using the common pump to fill the water bucket. Then back up three flights of stairs to the Conner apartment.

She thought she remembered how much water and how much oatmeal Ma used, but the oatmeal was stiff and gummy by the time she dished it up into three bowls. She glared at Carlotta and Davey, daring them to complain. They both ate silently.

Peggy and Carlotta took down the laundry strung up around the apartment and folded it into a basket. The basket was heavy. Both she and Carlotta would need to lug the basket down the stairs and deliver it to the house on Baxter Street. But she couldn't leave Davey alone. He would need to tag along with them.

The Conner children silently trudged down Mulberry, turned the corner to the "Five Points Intersection," then up Baxter. Peggy took the coins the lady of the house gave her, then shepherded Carlotta and Davey back home.

A basket of dirty clothes was waiting for them on the landing outside their apartment door.

It took Peggy and Carlotta five trips each with the water buckets to haul enough water up the stairs to fill the big copper washtub on the stove that Ma used to boil clothes. Peggy used a scrubboard and a bar of hard soap to scrub collars and dirty hems. Then another five trips for the rinse water.

She sent Carlotta down the stairs with the laundry money to wait for the milk wagon that came by around noon. They didn't often have milk, but Ma bought it about once a week. The milk was warm, but still sweet. Peggy smiled as Davey gulped his cupful and came up with milk all over his upper lip. Her smile hid a nagging sense of guilt. Would Da be mad that she spent the money for milk? Oh, how she wished Ma were here to tell her what to do!

By the time the rinsed laundry was hanging on the clotheslines strung about the main room, the light was failing. "Are we going to school?" Carlotta asked in a small voice.

Peggy shook her head. "Gotta fix supper for Da. Maybe tomorrow, when we're used to it a little more."

Peggy wondered how much of the precious few hunks of coal she should use for the supper fire. She dropped in two. When the fire was hot, she cut up some shriveled potatoes, carrots, and cabbage, filled the pot with water, and scooped in a little salt.

Darkness filled the apartment, and Peggy had to light the lard-oil lamp. The wick sputtered. The lard oil was almost gone.

The three children ate their supper of boiled vegetables and waited for their stepfather to come home. Peggy carefully moved the supper pot to a place on the cookstove where it would keep warm.

Night sounds and laughter, loud voices and

mothers yelling for their kids to come inside, but no footsteps on the stairway outside their door.

Davey fell asleep in his clothes. Peggy and Carlotta washed up the dishes, swept the floor, and waited. Their mother's absence filled the quiet space until it seemed as if even the walls were hurting.

Peggy's eyes drooped . . . then darted open at the knock on the door. Da was home at last. He would be so glad they had saved supper for him . . . if he wasn't drunk. With both eagerness and apprehension, she slid back the bolt and opened the door.

It wasn't her stepfather. Instead, Rev. Brace stood on the narrow landing, his short, pointed beard tilted in fatherly concern, a question behind his kind eyes as they searched the room for the man who wasn't there.

Peggy left the door open and turned away. Without a word she took an empty potato sack and began filling it with Davey's clothes. Another sack for Carlotta's. Finally her own. She took down her mother's shawl from its peg and folded it carefully into the sack.

Her hot, dry eyes caught Rev. Brace's, and he nodded in understanding as he picked up the sleeping Davey.

Mike Conner wasn't coming back.

Chapter 4

No Place Like Home

A rumbling sound startled Kip O'Reilly into wakefulness, and he opened his eyes. The damp, moldy ceiling of the holding cell in the police station stared back at him.

The rumbling sound rose and fell—a drunk brought in last night, snoring blissfully in a corner of the cell. Kip sat up, sore and stiff from sleeping on the hard floor. The mattress in the cellar of the tenement on Mulberry Street was more comfortable than *this*. And less smelly. At least he and his gang of street rovers could use the privies behind the big crowded tenements. Here in the  holding cell, nine street rovers of varying ages—ten, now, with the drunk—had to use one slop bucket, which just sat there stinking.

Two days he'd been here! Kip smacked his forehead with his hand, then his shoulders sagged. How stupid to get caught—by that fat ol' greengrocer, of all people. Kip had only lifted his daily breakfast from the barrels outside the shop—a handful of crackers, salted fish, or a big sour pickle. Nothing the man would really miss. It'd make more sense if he'd gotten caught lifting those shoes—five pairs of 'em— he'd picked up for his rovers last winter. Now, *that* was a notable bit of thievery: five sturdy pairs of shoes for his boys with a bit of room to grow in.

The other rovers and thieves in the cell began to stir. A surly fifteen-year-old caught picking the pockets of his shoeshine customers banged his tin cup against the bars of the cell yelling, "Water!" A couple of young gamblers yawned, then started up their dice game where they'd left off the night before when the lights were blown out.

A guard yelled for the cup-banger to shut up. But soon two policemen arrived with a bucket of water and a basket of bread. Nine hands each snatched a hunk of bread for himself. There was one left. With a sneering glance at the snoring drunk, the surly pickpocket reached for the remaining bread.

"Don't touch that bread," Kip growled.

The bigger boy barked a short laugh. "Ya tellin' *me* what ta do, ya little Mick? I'll take it if I wants!"

"No ya won't." Kip's tone was full of warning. He jerked his chin in the direction of the sleeping drunk. "That's his'n."

"Huh! Don't seem like he wants it, do he? And who are you, gettin' all high 'n mighty. They didn't throw ya in here 'cause ya was singin' in a church choir, now, did they?"

Kip moved between the big boy and the bread-basket. "Ain't s'posed ta steal from each other. If we don't look out fer each other, who gonna do it?"

"Huh. I look out fer myself."

"Well, *we* lookin' out fer *him* . . . ain't we?" Kip glared at the others in the cell. Inside he was quaking. These weren't his rovers. Maybe they didn't abide by the rules of the street. Maybe he was setting himself up for a good beating—and there was no place to run.

"Sure we is," said one of the dice players. "Back off, big boy. Ya got yer bread. What makes ya think *you* got a right ta that bread any more 'n the rest of us? Or do ya want to fight *us* fer it?"

Kip swallowed the grin that threatened to spoil his stare-down with the bigger boy. Wouldn't do to gloat.

But as he sat back down and tore hunks out of his bread with his teeth, worry about his situation made it difficult to swallow. How long was he going to be cooped up here in this jail? *Two days already*. Did his rovers know where he was? Even if they did, what could they do? And if he didn't get out, what would happen to them? Billy was only nine, Ned and Smack about ten, and Hooter maybe eleven. They all looked up to Kip, who'd taken them under his wing.

"O'Reilly?" yelled a guard. "Which one o' you cats is O'Reilly?"

Kip frowned. What did they want with him?

"Sergeant wants ta see ya," said the burly guard. "Move along now, ain't got all day."

Kip didn't know whether to be glad or worried. Either they were letting him go . . . or they were taking him to Tombs Prison. But he gave a cocky wave to the sad lot in the holding cell. At least he was out of *there*.

But when he walked into the station room, the first person he saw was the greengrocer, scowling like he'd eaten one of his own sour pickles. Uh-oh. This didn't look good.

Then Kip heard another familiar voice. "Sergeant, may I have a word with the boy before you hear our motion?" Startled, Kip's eyes darted around the room until he found the speaker. Rev. Brace rose from a chair and motioned to Kip.

"Rev!" said Kip in a big whisper. "What are *you* doin' here?"

Rev. Brace lifted an eyebrow. "What are *you* doing here is the question. But never mind that now. I have a proposition to make to you."

"Me, sir?" Kip glanced uneasily over his shoulder at the greengrocer. If that fat man wanted him indentured to work off his thieving . . . well, he wouldn't do it. He wasn't going to be anybody's servant, no sir.

Rev. Brace's face was grave. "Mr. Fry here is inclined to press charges against you. He says you're a repeat offender and a confirmed thief and should be locked up."

Kip's mouth dropped. "Aw, Rev, that ain't true. I

mean, I do help myself to a bit o' breakfast on a reg'lar basis, but cain't be no harm in that. Only a few crackers from the top o' the barrel—and such a big barrel at that!"

"Mmm. That's not the point. You are taking what doesn't belong to you. That's stealing, and it's against the law—man's law and God's law. But . . . I believe you're a good boy at heart, Kip O'Reilly. I've spoken with Mr. Fry, and he's willing to drop the charges on one condition."

Kip looked warily at Rev. Brace. "What kind o' condition?"

"That you come to stay in our Boys' Lodging House and be responsible to the Children's Aid Society."

"Aw, I cain't do that, Rev. What about me boys?— Billy an' the rest. Besides . . ." Kip drew himself up. "I make my own way. Don't take no charity."

"Who's talking about charity?" Rev. Brace's voice was crisp, businesslike. "We charge six cents per night for a bed; four cents for supper. Bath is thrown in free. You can keep your newspaper job for the time being—till you find something with more future. It'll help pay your expenses. As for the rest of the boys— they're welcome, too. Same terms. Ten cents a day room and board." Rev. Brace leaned closer and dropped his voice. "Don't think too long, Kip. Your other choice is six months in jail."

✧ ✧ ✧ ✧

Kip took a deep breath outside the police station. The Rev was right. It wasn't too hard to make up his mind. Besides, if he didn't like it, he could just leave whenever he liked . . . and if the police wanted him then, they'd have to catch him first.

As they headed back toward Five Points, Kip and Rev. Brace passed the corner of Canal and Centre. The boy with red hair was hawking papers. "Git yer *Times* right here!"

"Hey!" Kip yelled. "This here's *my*—"

He was cut off by Rev. Brace, who pulled him farther down the street. "Don't fight it, Kip. You'll get your job back, all right, but working another corner might be best. After all, didn't some of your customers see you getting nabbed by the police? I'd keep a low profile if I were you—build up some new customers on another corner."

Kip glared at the other newsboy over his shoulder. He didn't like giving up his corner so easy—especially to Red. His pride made him want to take it back.

Just then a flurry of wings and feathers beat around his head. A moment later, Pogo landed on Kip's shoulder. "Hey!" Kip laughed. "Lookee here, Rev. It's Pogo!"

"I see," said Rev. Brace dryly. But an amused smile twitched under his mustache.

"Say, Rev, can I take Pogo with me ta the Lodging House? Look here—he's been waitin' fer me two days! I feel kinda responsible fer 'im. It'd mean a great deal ta me, sir."

"Now, Kip, you know we can't have a pigeon in

the Lodging House."

"Don't mean *in* the Lodging House, sir. I'll feed 'im out on the street—just so he knows where ta find me." Kip felt in his pocket. A few kernels of corn remained. "He won't be a nuisance, I promise."

"Hmph. Never met a pigeon that *wasn't* a nuisance," Rev. Brace muttered. But Kip noticed that he didn't say no.

They stopped by the tenement on Mulberry Street, but none of Kip's boys were around. "Not s'prised." Kip tried not to be worried. "They all out doin' business. I'll come back later ta find them."

"No, *I* will come back later to find them. Half an hour ago you agreed to be responsible to the Children's Aid Society in exchange for jail time. So that's where we're going."

Kip stuck his hands in his pockets and followed Rev. Brace reluctantly. He didn't like people telling him what to do, not even the Rev, who always had a good heart for the street rovers. Well, he'd just have to make the best of it . . . for now.

Pogo did his best to stay on Kip's shoulder, flapping his wings in protest when his human transportation turned this corner, then that. When they arrived at 683 Broadway, Kip took the last small handful of corn out of his pocket and threw it on the sidewalk for Pogo as they stepped inside.

In the big room where he and the rovers had come for the Boys' Meeting, Kip saw a group of children—mostly girls—and a plump woman with her hair pulled back into a bun clustered around two well-made satchels. One of the girls in a starchy-clean pinafore looked up. "Oh, Rev. Brace, look here! Miss Wilson finally sent our clothes over."

Rev. Brace nodded gravely, but his eyes had a twinkle. "Good, good. . . . Uh, Mrs. Delaney, could I have a word with you?"

Rev. Brace and the matron stepped out of the room and headed for the office. Kip stood there awkwardly, hands shoved in his pockets. He noticed a little boy looking at him. With a wink, Kip took a penny out of his pocket, showed it to the little boy, then tossed it in the air. He caught it, slapped his hand on the back of his other hand, then lifted his hand to show that the penny had disappeared.

The little boy's eyes grew wide, and he ran over to Kip, mouth open. The biggest girl in the group followed him. "Say, I know you," she said. "My ma—" Her voice caught. "My ma did washin' for yer rovers, and ya brought her coal. I'm Peggy Conner. And this here's Davey."

Relief at seeing familiar faces from Mulberry Street sparked a grin on Kip's face. He squatted down until he was at eye level with the little boy. "My name's Kip. What you doin' here, little man?"

Davey hung his head. "Mama died." His lip quivered.

"Mrs. Conner? The washerwoman?" Kip straightened up and looked at Peggy. "My eyes, I'm more'n sorry ta hear that."

He felt Davey tug on his pants. "Are ya the boy what's gonna be my big brother at the Lodgin' House?"

Kip shot a quick look at Peggy. She shrugged. "Rev. Brace told Davey he was bringin' him a big brother ta look after him. Matron says he can't stay with the girls."

Kip straightened. The Rev sure was taking liberty planning his life. A girlish voice suddenly rose in distress from the direction of the satchels. "Muffin's not here, Lauren! She didn't send Muffin!"

Peggy jerked her head toward the sound. "That's Lauren and Lena. Come on an' meet the others."

Kip recognized Peggy's little sister, Carlotta, dressed similarly to Peggy in well-worn homespun. But the other two girls digging through the satchels . . . what were a couple of swells doing at the Children's Aid Society? And why did they look familiar?

"Oh!" The girl named Lauren looked at him in awe. "Aren't you the boy who sells papers? Lena, look—it's the boy with the pet pigeon!"

Kip remembered them now. The two sisters walking with the lady in brown, just before the greengrocer gave chase. His ears reddened.

Hero worship shone in Davey's eyes. "Ya got a pet pigeon?"

"Yeah, I do. He's outside waitin' fer me. Wanna see 'im do some tricks?" Kip grabbed Davey's hand and smiled an invitation to Lauren and Lena. But Lena turned away, her mouth pulled down at the corners.

Odd, thought Kip as Davey dragged him toward the door. Lena was the one who'd been so excited over Pogo the other day. Why didn't she want to see his pet pigeon now?

As Davey pulled him outside, Kip made a promise to himself: He was going to put a smile on that little pinched face.

Chapter 5

Off the Streets

"Mornin', Mr. Tibbs. Need a hand with those papers there?" Kip O'Reilly tried to make his voice sound neither timid nor cocky as he stroked the velvety nose of the newspaper horse. He knew he had to handle Tibbs just right in order to get his job back.

Tibbs kept unloading bundles of the *Times* as he glared at Kip. "Ya got nerve, boy, showin' up after cheatin' me outa twenty-five papers last Tuesday."

"That's what I come ta see ya about, Mr. Tibbs." Unasked, Kip began unloading the newspaper wagon hitched to the patient horse dozing at the curb. "Didn't mean ta cheat ya. Had an emergency—"

Tibbs snorted. "Emergency, my foot. The boy what took over

yer corner heard that the police got hold o' ya."

Kip winced. The truth was out. He'd have to deal with it. "I know it sounds bad, sir, but I come back ta make it up ta ya." He lugged out more bundles of papers till Tibbs held up his hand. The rest had to go to another drop-off.

"Make it up, huh? Well, ya owes me fer twenty-five papers, nickel apiece . . . that's a dollar twenty-five."

Kip's heart sank. He dug into his pocket for the ten nickels he'd collected Tuesday morning before the police chased him off. But that left seventy-five cents he still owed Mr. Tibbs for the fifteen papers he'd just dropped on the street when he ran. Tibbs owed him back ten cents—a penny a paper—for the ten he'd sold. But the man would probably keep it to pay down Kip's debt. How was he supposed to get the ten cents he needed for his room and supper at the Lodging House?

For a moment Kip wavered. He felt hemmed in, saddled by the burden of honesty. Maybe he should just round up his rovers and disappear into another section of the city. Wouldn't be hard . . .

But something held him. The Rev had gone to bat for him, getting him out of jail. And little Davey needed someone to look out for him at the Boys' Lodging House. Couldn't let the little guy down, not after losing his ma so sudden. Kip let out a big sigh. It'd take a while, but once he paid off Mr. Tibbs the noose wouldn't feel so tight. He'd promised the Rev he'd quit thieving. Well, he'd give it a try.

Tibbs finally agreed to give Kip ten cents a day from

what he sold and keep the rest of his profit until the debt was paid. Kip took twenty-five papers, toyed with the temptation to fight for his old corner at Canal and Centre, but finally headed west toward Broadway.

The corner of Broadway and Walker was alive with traffic. Broadway ran north toward the heart of New York City and the upscale neighborhoods. Covered carriages and hansom cabs clattered past on the cobblestone streets, along with wagons piled high with sacks and barrels.

Kip sold out his twenty-five papers and headed back to the drop-off to wait for Mr. Tibbs to settle up the day's accounts. While Tibbs was busy with another newsboy, Kip slyly helped himself to the last of the corn in the feed bag. "You don't mind, do ya, boy," he whispered to the dozing horse. He headed back to the Lodging House, whistling. He had ten cents in his pocket for a decent bed and a hot meal that night. Not bad. Not bad at all.

As Kip skirted a mound of garbage and turned down Baxter, three youthful bodies suddenly rose up from a dark doorway. Hooter, Ned, and Billy stood silently in his path, staring reproachfully.

Kip wanted to shout with glee—but where was Smack?

"Where ya been, Kip?" said Hooter. "Never thought ya'd run out on yer boys."

He felt guilty—but that made him mad. What did he have to feel guilty about? "I didn't run out on ya! Look here . . ." Kip explained about getting hauled to jail by the police until liberated by Rev. Brace. "The

Rev told me he'd find you boys and tell ya ta come on to the Lodging House, too."

"He told us." More sullen stares.

"We don't want ta get shut up in no 'sylum."

"Thought ya liked bein' a rover, Kip."

"Ya gotta come back, Kip. We lost—" Billy's face fell.

"You lost what?" Kip demanded.

Hooter sidled forward. "We cain't find Smack. We was all down at the docks, spread-out like, doin' odd jobs ta get some fish . . . but Smack disappeared. First you, then Smack. We been lookin' fer ya both fer two days. Don't have no money, no food. You said no thievin' 'cause we might get caught. But what else can we do? Tell me that, Kip!"

Kip felt the walls closing in on him again. He'd promised the Rev, but . . . he couldn't just leave his rovers to fend for themselves on the streets, could he? Smack was missing, and the others needed someone to prod them. Or what if bigger rovers like that bad egg in the jail took advantage of them?

"Here." Kip impulsively pulled the ten cents out of his pocket and thrust it at Hooter. "It's all I got, but it'll get ya some bread. But I ain't got no choice right now, boys. The Rev made me promise ta get off the street if I wanted out o' jail. Besides, the Boys' Lodging House ain't no 'sylum. Gotta pay yer way." He gripped Hooter by the shoulder and pulled him aside. "Get Billy shoe shinin' with Ned, Hooter. See if ya can sell papers. Get some money in yer pockets and come on over ta the Society. Hot supper, four cents; bed fer six. Warm an' dry, too. We could be together that way."

Hooter shrugged and looked at his shoes.

"Well, ya know where ta find me." Kip hated to leave the boys standing in the street, but he stuck his hands in his pockets and forced a nonchalant whistle as he headed back to his new "home." They'd come around . . . he hoped.

The Boys' Lodging House was located in a different block than the Children's Aid Society, where the girls were staying. Kip swung by the Society, like he'd promised, to pick up Davey Conner. Davey's sisters had been taking care of him that morning. The gray-and-white pigeon was strutting back and forth in front of the door, looking this way and that.

"Are ya gonna feed Pogo now, Kip?" asked Davey eagerly as he came outside.

"He better not." Rev. Brace came out of his office and joined the Conner children, the Rogers sisters, and Kip clustered on the sidewalk. Rev. Brace rolled his eyes. "Mrs. Delaney will have my hide if she has to scrub pigeon droppings off these steps."

The girls giggled. All except Lena.

"No problem, Rev . . . uh, Reverend, sir," Kip said cheerfully. "I'll just save this corn till we gets over ta the Lodging House."

"Hmm. Say, Kip, where do you get the corn for your pigeon?"

Kip grinned. "Horse friend o' mine lets me nip it—long as his owner ain't watchin'."

Rev. Brace shook his head. "Can't *do* that, Kip.

You promised. No stealing."

"Aw, Rev, it's just horse feed!"

"That's the rule, Kip. You could *ask*, or offer to pay, or buy a sack of corn yourself from the feedstore."

"But I ain't got no money today, Rev. Ran into my boys . . . they was hungry." He glanced resentfully at the girls who were witnessing his humiliation.

Rev. Brace's eyebrows went up. He drew Kip aside. "You gave your money away, Kip? That's very generous . . . but you still need ten cents to pay for your supper and room tonight. You said yourself you don't want charity."

"But—!" Frustration boiled inside Kip. Life sure was a whole lot simpler as a street rover.

✧ ✧ ✧ ✧

Kip and Rev. Brace worked out a plan where Kip got "paid" for looking after Davey and doing errands for Mrs. Delaney till he got his debt to Mr. Tibbs paid off and could begin paying for his bed and supper in cash. Then, a few days later, Hooter, Ned, and Billy showed up at the Lodging House, each clutching four pennies, which they plunked down for a hot supper of boiled potatoes, cabbage, and sausage.

"No sign o' Smack yet?" Kip asked Hooter. Hooter shook his head. A worry knot tightened in Kip's head, but he had to grin watching Billy close his eyes in sheer bliss as he sucked noisily on the juicy sausage.

Davey poked Kip. "Are they goin' ta stay here?"

"Not me!" snorted Hooter. "I heard ya gotta

take a *bath*."

But Kip grinned slyly. "Soon, Davey. Soon."

Sure enough, within a week Hooter, Ned, and Billy forked over six cents each for the privilege of sleeping in a real bed at the Boys' Lodging House.

Hooter had signed up with Mr. Tibbs as a newsboy and was selling papers over on Bowery. He passed on his kit of boot-black, brushes, and rags to Billy and Ned, who set up "shop" near a cabstand to shine shoes while people waited for a cab.

Their first night in the Lodging House, a cold May drizzle slicked the cobblestones outside and seeped into all the broken windows and damp basements of the Five Points district—a fact that eased the indignities of a good hard scrubbing with soap and rag. "Sure glad I ain't bummin' tonight," whispered Billy, his thin body wrapped gratefully in a warm wool blanket. Full stomachs and warm beds lulled the ragtag little gang into an early sleep.

Kip said nothing, just kept whittling on a piece of cedar in the low lamplight, feeling an unfamiliar happiness that he and his boys and little Davey Conner were all safe tonight. All except Smack. Thinking of Smack, a tiny fear licked the edges of his happiness. Nothing good in his life ever lasted long.

✧ ✧ ✧ ✧

As word got around the streets about the Boys' Lodging House, more and more street rovers turned up each evening for the hot meals and beds. Mr. Tracey became its full-time superintendent, and Kip was relieved that the man never again mentioned that the Bible lesson at the first Boys' Meeting had turned into a near riot.

As May turned to June that summer of 1854, the

relentless heat seemed to bake right into the rough cobblestone streets and tall brick tenements, which failed to cool off at night. The newsboys called out the headlines—"Missouri Compromise Repealed in Kansas!" . . . "San Francisco Fears More Earthquakes!" . . . "Indian Agent Negotiates Land Deals for Railroad!"—without understanding or caring about the stories swelling like tidal waves across the states and territories. Headlines were nothing to the boys compared to day-by-day survival on the streets of New York.

Once Kip got his debt to Mr. Tibbs paid off, Rev. Brace talked to him about putting some of his money in a "savings bank" at the Lodging House. Kip got suspicious. Who ever heard of hiding your money when you could spend it? But Rev. Brace explained paid interest—money making money. Kip wasn't sure he understood. But the clincher was that Rev. Brace said he could have it back anytime he wanted.

Six-year-old Davey Conner was declared too young to have to earn his keep, so Kip took him each morning to the Children's Aid Society to be cared for by his sisters and the Rogers girls, then picked him up again when it was time to return to the Lodging House. Not having to wonder where his supper was going to come from gave Kip something he'd never had before: time to think. After getting Davey in bed, he often sat whittling with his pocketknife—the one he'd won off another rover a year or two back—while the other boys crowded in corners to tell street stories or toss dice when the "super" wasn't looking.

Kip was a familiar figure at the main office of the Society because of Davey. Living on the streets most of his life with a gang of rovers, the only girls Kip had known were street urchins like himself. The younger ones, their noses running, their hair matted, sold flowers or matches or swept sidewalks to earn a penny or two. The older ones usually ended up dancing in the taverns—unless the Rev got hold of them. Kip had to respect the plump Mrs. Delaney, who handled all the "strays" Rev. Brace rounded up and took to the Children's Aid Society. The bigger street girls had mouths as rude and rough as the street rovers—sometimes rougher.

But Peggy Conner was different. Kip admired the way the girl held her chin up and took charge of Davey and Carlotta, and even the misplaced Rogers girls. The girl was tough, not rough.

But those Rogers girls . . . they were head-scratchers. Imagine being dumped by their governess at the Society, while their parents were off seeing Paris or London or wherever rich people went. Kip thought the parents would show up one of these days and that would be the last the Society would see of the "poor little rich girls." Still, he was puzzled by the younger one—Lena. She rarely spoke and never smiled. He had tried to ask her about "Muffin"— Lauren had told him in a whisper that Muffin was a toy rabbit Lena had had since babyhood—but Lena just shook her head and turned away.

Animals. Kip was sure she liked animals, just like he did. He still remembered how excited she got over Pogo that day—though he reddened remembering how those rich girls watched him get chased by the greengrocer and caught by the police.

Kip held up the piece of wood he'd been whittling. No, Lena hadn't smiled . . . yet.

Chapter 6

Workshop or West?

With his knife and whittling safely stowed in his pocket, Kip knocked on Rev. Brace's office door at the Children's Aid Society. Rev. Brace had asked him to come by, said he wanted to talk about something. But standing at the office door, Kip was suddenly uneasy. Was he in trouble? He'd been *trying* to not do any thieving, but he just couldn't bring himself to *ask* Tibbs if he could nip some corn from his horse's feed bag, and a bag of feed cost a lot more than Kip ever had in his pocket. He tried to remember to save some of his supper bread for Pogo, but sometimes the feed bag just hanging there on the newspaper wagon was too tempting—

"Come in."

Kip snatched off his cap and stood facing a large desk cluttered with newspapers, ink bottles, pens, and stacks of paper with writing on them. Books sat on shelves and even in stacks on the floor. A big black Bible dominated one corner of the desk.

"Sit down, sit down." Rev. Brace made a tent with his fingers and pursed his lips thoughtfully. "Kip, how much do you make selling papers?"

Kip shrugged. "Penny a paper. Try to sell all twenty-five in the morning."

"You're what . . . thirteen? What are you going to do when you're sixteen, or twenty?"

Kip hesitated. "Sell papers, I guess. Don't know how ta do nothin' else." He brightened. "Bet I could do Mr. Tibbs' job—doing the drop-offs!"

"Mmmm." Rev. Brace frowned thoughtfully. "Kip, America is the land of opportunity. But most of the street rovers aren't prepared for opportunity. A lot of the rovers are good lads like yourself, given half a chance. But selling papers? Gets you a meal and a bed today, but won't take you anywhere tomorrow."

Kip said nothing. What was Rev. Brace talking about?

Rev. Brace became more businesslike. "I'm leaving in a few weeks for England; be gone a couple of months. But before I go, I'd like to start a workshop for the boys, Kip—maybe shoemaking, something that would teach them a trade."

"Gotta learn a trade, boy! Doin' this fer yer own good, now, ya hear? Don't ya go runnin' off, now, or I'll beat some sense into ya!" His father's last words

as he left young Kip at the shoe tanner's shop echoed in his head as Rev. Brace talked on.

Kip jumped up, anger rising in his chest. "Oh, I see it now. Yer just like all the rest of 'em, Rev. Sweet-talkin' the rovers, but ya just want slave labor in some sweatshop, doin' all the dirty work while the big cats take all the money. Well, I won't have it! I'm gonna get my rovers outa here and—"

"Kip! Kip!" Rev. Brace stood up, too, his eyes wide. "Whatever are you talking about?"

"Indenture, Rev! Just another word for slavin'." Kip spit out the words. "Spent six months in a shoe tanner's shop when I was eight. Didn't learn no trade. Didn't make no money. Just had to 'do this' and 'do that,' and a box on the ears if'n I was too slow. Would still be slavin' if I hadn't run away. Well, I won't do it! And I won't let my rovers do it, neither! I—"

"Kip!" Rev. Brace's voice was kind but firm. "I agree!"

Kip pulled his words up short. "You . . . agree?"

"Absolutely! No indenture. I'm talking about a workshop where the boys actually learn to make shoes, sell their product, and share the profits. Maybe set up their own shops someday. Yes, it would be hard work. Opportunity doesn't come easy. You've got to make your own opportunity. But . . ." Rev. Brace held out his hands. "A lot of the rovers will be thinking the same way you did. I need your help to encourage them to at least give it a try. What do you say? Will you at least hear me out?"

Kip slowly sat back down.

An hour later he left the office and was nearly tackled by Davey Conner. "Kip! I been waitin' fer ya. I thought ya forgot about me!"

"What? Me forget about ya, Davey? Naw, couldn't do that. Now, say . . . where would Lena be this time o' day?"

Davey gave him a bored look that said, *What do ya want with* her *fer, anyway?* But he obediently led Kip to where his sisters and the Rogers girls were peeling huge mounds of potatoes, while Mrs. Delaney chopped and talked.

"Could—could I see Lena a moment, Mrs. Delaney?"

The matron waved Lena off her stool, and the eight-year-old came slowly toward the boys. Kip knelt down on one knee so he could look Lena in the eyes. Reaching into his pocket, he drew out the piece of wood he'd been carving and held it toward Lena. "Here, I made this for you."

Lena's eyes widened as she looked at the carved wooden rabbit.

"I know it's not soft and cuddly like yer Muffin," Kip apologized. "Don't know how ta make one o' those. But thought ya could talk ta this here rabbit friend, just the same."

Lena reached out and took the carved rabbit with both hands. She stared at it a long time, then drew it close, rocking her body from side to side. Then she lifted her eyes to Kip's face. And smiled.

✧ ✧ ✧ ✧

Kip wasn't sure who had the tougher job. Rev. Brace said, "If you get the boys, I'll get the workshop." And sure enough, within a week Rev. Brace had rented a large room in a building on Wooster Street and had started writing pamphlets promoting his idea and contacting rich New Yorkers to equip it.

But convincing the street rovers was another story. "We get paid ever' day, like we do sellin' papers and shinin'?" Hooter wanted to know.

Kip thought about it. "Don't think so. Takes more time ta make a pair o' shoes than it does ta shine 'em."

"Then what good is it?" "How we gonna pay fer our supper and this here bed?" "Can we cut out if'n we don't like it?" "Pickin' a few pockets seems a whole sight easier." The last was greeted by general hoots of laughter.

Kip had no answers to their questions. But after talking to Rev. Brace, he had learned a new word: the *future*. "Well, you rovers do what ya want," he said stubbornly. "But I ain't aimin' ta sell the *Times* for a penny a paper when I'm grown, and I don't like the idea o' ending up in the Tombs fer picking a few pockets. I say we give the workshop a fair go."

By the time the shoemaking workshop was ready to go, forty boys showed up.

At first, enthusiasm was high. Mr. Rollins, the shoemaker Rev. Brace had employed to teach his craft, worked patiently with the boys, teaching them how to handle the leather and the tools. To begin, he showed the boys how to measure each other's feet and let them practice pegging soles for their own pair of shoes. Kip drank in the smell of the leather—it smelled of the mysterious land of cowboys and Indians far beyond New York. His eyes caressed the knives and awls, each with their own special task. But actually getting the tools to do the right thing and make the right cut was harder than it looked. A lot more leather ended up on the scrap heap than in a pair of wearable shoes.

And the days were long. If it was hot on the sun-baked street corners hawking newspapers in the morning, it was twice as hot inside the workshop on Wooster in the afternoon. "We're goin' down ta the docks today, Kip," said Hooter one day as they settled up accounts with Mr. Tibbs at the newspaper drop-off. "Wanna come?"

Kip hesitated only a moment. The shoes he was working on would be there tomorrow. But today was one of those rare days in July, when the breezes brought clean air from the rivers through the Lower East Side. And it wasn't like he would lose any money today by going to the docks instead. They had yet to see any money for their work—and Mr. Rollins said they wouldn't, either, until they had some work he could sell.

The next day Kip showed up at the workshop—but the room was half empty. A lot of the half-finished work sat idle. Mr. Rollins, the shoemaker, was waving his hands and talking in a loud voice to Mr. Smith, the keen young man who was acting director of the Children's Aid Society while Rev. Brace was in Europe. Kip bent over his unfinished shoes at one of the worktables, wondering if Rollins had told Smith he had skipped out yesterday.

"This isn't going to work, Mr. Smith." Rollins was agitated. "Look around . . . how many boys do we have today? Fifteen . . . maybe sixteen? Yesterday only ten showed up! We can't run a business like that!"

Kip leaned hard on the knife in his hand, trying to cut through the thick leather.

"You're absolutely right, Mr. Rollins. But we must give it a little more time—at least until Rev. Brace returns. These boys are used to living from day to day on the streets. They haven't been taught the virtues of responsibility and self-control. Most live without hope—no wonder they find it hard to stick with something long term."

"Hmph. Brace hired me to teach shoemaking. I can't baby-sit forty boys and teach them the ABCs of life at the same time."

Kip scowled and pressed harder on the knife. What did these *gentlemen* know about life? Did they know what it was like going to sleep hungry? Sleeping on a steam grate? Ask a street rover about life! A street rover had to live by his wits. A street rover could teach the swells a thing or—*snap*!

"Ow!" Kip yelled. He stared at the broken knife handle in his hand. The knife blade had flipped up and stabbed his other hand. Blood welled up from the small wound and trickled onto the stubborn leather.

The two men strode instantly to his side. Mr.

Smith whipped out his handkerchief and gave it to Kip to
press against the cut. But Mr. Rollins was steaming.
"See that, Smith? Now we've got to replace a per-
fectly good tool. No-shows . . . carelessness . . . this
do-gooder project is going to end up costing more
money than it ever earns." Rollins stomped off, bark-
ing at first one boy and then another as he examined
their work.

"You all right, Kip? . . . No, keep the handkerchief; tie it around the cut."

Kip watched Mr. Smith head for the door, with a

wave at the boys on his way out. Smith was all right—but Kip would be glad when Rev. Brace got back from England.

The cut had stopped bleeding. Kip started to stuff the handkerchief in his pocket, but then stopped. He eyed the broken knife. Careless, was he? An idea began to form in his mind. He'd show them what he could do. Wrapping the blade of the knife and the broken handle in the handkerchief, he slipped them into his pocket.

✧ ✧ ✧ ✧

As street rovers and newsboys from all over the Five Points area dove into their plates of rice and beans that evening, Kip noticed Mr. Smith talking to Superintendent Tracey. Telling Davey he would be right back, Kip pushed through the noisy throng of boys toward the two men.

"Brace is right! Institutional life simply doesn't teach a boy what he needs to know," Mr. Smith was saying as Kip approached. "We provide a bed, we provide food, and we're trying to teach some a trade. But a boy needs a mentor, a father figure, to discipline him, teach him responsibility and moral values, all the everyday skills and manners that help a young person become a productive citizen."

Superintendent Tracey threw up his hands. "There are almost ninety boys here! That kind of guidance takes a family, Mr. Smith! Something these boys don't have."

"Exactly," murmured Smith, rubbing his chin thoughtfully. "Exactly what Rev. Brace was talking about before he left. . . ."

"Uh, Mr. Smith?" Kip held out the rumpled handkerchief. "I wanted ta return this. I'm sorry it got all, well . . ."

"What? Oh yes, yes. Quite all right." Mr. Smith took the bloody handkerchief and stuck it absently into his pocket. "Think about it, man," he continued to Tracey, as if Kip had not interrupted. "America is expanding west, with space enough and food enough for everyone. And yet where do the immigrant poor reside? In our crowded cities!"

"But these children are orphans and homeless! There's no way—"

"No way?" Smith laughed. "If the American farm family holds the solution to the problem of New York's homeless children, Charles Loring Brace will surely find a way! But," Smith shrugged, "in the meantime, he left us to carry on. So carry on we must . . . right, Kip?" Smith slapped Kip on the shoulder good-naturedly as he turned to go.

Supper was almost over when Superintendent Tracey clapped for attention. "Quiet, please! Quiet! I have a job opportunity here for an ambitious boy."

Kip looked up from his plate. A job? Might be better than shoemaking.

"A gentleman called me today," said the superintendent, "wanting an office boy. The pay would be three dollars a week—"

Hands shot up all over the room. "Me!" "Let me

go!" "Me, sir!"

Three dollars a week? That was twice as much as he had been making selling papers. Kip stood up. "I'd like that job, Mr. Tracey."

Mr. Tracey cleared his throat. "This gentleman needs a boy who can write."

The waving hands slowly lowered. Kip felt like a fool for standing. Slowly he sat down.

Mr. Tracey looked around the room at the disappointed faces. "Well, now, don't be discouraged. Suppose we start a night school after supper and learn to write."

Kip eyed Hooter, Ned, and Billy. So far the rovers had balked at the idea of school. But if learning to write meant three dollars a week . . .

"I'm in!" Kip hollered. All around the room a general cry went up. "We're in!"

✧ ✧ ✧ ✧

The first lesson that night was spent copying letters of the alphabet. To show them how the letters spelled words, the superintendent also wrote the word *cat* and let them copy it. It didn't matter what age the boys were—most of them had never been inside a schoolroom, so they were all starting at the beginning.

Light still lingered outside when the boys finished their first writing lesson. Kip and Davey joined the other boys who gathered outside to sit on the stoop of the old building that harbored the Lodging

House. While Davey idly tossed bits of rice saved from supper to the demanding Pogo, Kip pulled out his pocketknife and started whittling on another piece of cedar.

"Ya makin' another toy rabbit?" Davey asked hopefully.

"Nope." Kip kept whittling, thinking about the conversation he'd overheard. What kind of crazy scheme was the Rev thinking up now? Kip snorted. That man did more thinking than the rest of New York put together. But . . . families for the rovers? Out West?

Well, it didn't matter anyway, since he'd never really had one. Davey, now . . . he'd had a mother and a stepfather, and he still had sisters. And the Rogers girls still had parents . . . somewhere. Maybe being orphans was harder on them because they knew what they were missing. Maybe the Rev would find families for them. Well, that'd be good.

The pocketknife bit deeper into the wood. But it was too late for him. He'd have to find that "future" the Rev kept talking about some other way.

Chapter 7

The Orphan Train

W hat's this?" Mr. Rollins took the knife Kip held out to him a week later. The blade was the familiar "leather cutter" used by all the boys in the workshop. But the handle . . .

"I made a new handle for the one I broke." Kip held his breath. Making the handle hadn't been too hard. But attaching blade and handle into a sturdy, useable knife had made him sweat. He had saved the brass pins from the old handle, but making the holes just the right size so the pins stayed snug and tight took hours.

Mr. Rollins turned it over several times. "Amazing . . ." he murmured. "Well, try it out. See how it works." He handed the

knife back to Kip, then called the rest of the boys together and began demonstrating how to punch holes for laces.

As usual, the workshop was sweltering, even with all the windows open. Not a day went by that Kip wasn't tempted to head for the docks or find a cool basement rather than show up for work—especially work that hadn't paid a penny yet, as the boys were still learning the trade. But the night school was having a strange effect. After just a week, Kip could write his own name. And he was beginning to recognize words on store windows, on signs, and even in the newspaper: *street . . . hat . . . go . . . come . . . war . . .*

Suddenly he was excited by a new reality: *He could learn new things!* Even the workshop held a new fascination. "Shoemaking" as a trade did little to hold his interest. But the actual process of making shoes was broken down into many interesting parts— what leather did when you soaked it in water and shaped it around a wooden foot form . . . how to cut leather to make it curve without wrinkles . . . how to stitch together two pieces of leather of different weights . . . how many applications of linseed oil made leather soft and supple . . . the many ways to join different types of materials—pegging, glue, laces, nails, stitching. Kip was so interested in the many different parts that he was almost taken by surprise with his first finished product: a shoe!

"Look! Look, Mr. Rollins! I made a pair o' shoes— and they fit!" Kip pulled on the ankle-high shoes and did an Irish jig between two workshop tables.

"Excellent, my boy!" chuckled a familiar voice. "I, too, have some happy news."

Startled, Kip looked up. "Rev! I didn't know ya was back! Look at what . . ." Kip's words trailed off. For the first time he noticed a pretty young woman in a day cap tied under her chin, wearing a full crinoline dress that barely fit between the work-tables. One hand was tucked coyly in the crook of Rev. Brace's arm.

"Mr. Rollins . . . boys . . ." Rev. Brace's mustache could not hide his wide grin. "I'd like to introduce my wife, Mrs. Brace. Letitia, these are some of the boys I've been telling you about."

The new Mrs. Brace smiled at the sea of open mouths and blinking eyes. "Charles talks of nothing else. Almost makes a girl jealous." Her eyes twinkled and she bent over to look at Kip's feet. "Those shoes are grand, young man."

Kip's face went red. What could he say?

Rev. Brace took a newspaper from under his arm. "That's my good news. I'm afraid I also have some news that isn't so good." He turned to a small article inside and began to read. " 'The recent invention of a "pegging machine" promises to move the shoemaking trade out of the last century into the next.' "

Kip found his voice. "What's it mean, sir?"

Mr. Rollins slapped a worktable. "It means that newfangled machine is going to put this workshop out of business, that's what. If that don't beat all."

"But can't we just get one o' them machines—and

make the work go faster?" Kip asked.

"Problem is," said Rev. Brace, "that machine is going to replace workers—which means they can make more shoes with fewer people. But we need a workshop that can put *more*, not less, of you rovers to work."

❖ ❖ ❖ ❖

Most rovers were glad when the workshop shut down and happily went back to running the streets. Kip wasn't sure how he felt. He'd stuck it out—well, mostly—even though he never did take a shine to shoemaking as a trade. But he liked knowing there were new things to learn—and that he could master them.

The last day the workshop was open, Mr. Rollins had handed him the leather cutter with the hand-made handle. *"Keep it, son. That was smart thinking. You've got a good head on your shoulders."* But he'd walked away shaking his head, muttering, *"What a waste . . ."*

Kip felt restless. Selling papers didn't give him that same cocky feeling anymore. Used to be, put a little change in his pocket and he felt like king of the world. But the Rev was right: There was no future in it. What kind of future did he have, anyway?

September brought relief from the unrelenting heat of summer. Kip picked up his daily papers, gave Tibbs' patient bay a friendly scratch, and took up his corner on Broadway. "Read all about it! 'Kansas Bleedin' Over Slavery'! . . . 'French Join Brits in

Crimean War'! Get yer *Times* right here!" To his amazement, Kip could read some of the words straight off the newspaper for himself—night school at the Lodging House was starting to pay off. But it only increased his restlessness. Here he was, selling news stories about things happening way out in the Wild West, even on the other side of the world—and he'd never traveled farther than Twenty-Second Street.

A hopeful stray dog trailed Kip back to the newspaper drop-off. Kip helped himself to the last bit of corn from the ever-ready feed bag and gave Tibbs' horse another pat. "Pogo says thanks," he whispered in the horse's ear as he took off down Centre Street. The dog was still following him.

"Hey, boy." Kip stopped and scratched the scrawny mutt behind the ears. "Don't look at me—I ain't got nothin' fer ya, unless ya like horse feed."

A cab horse trotted past, and suddenly the driver pulled up. "Kip! Kip O'Reilly. Just the boy I wanted to see." Rev. Brace leaned out of the carriage window and waved Kip over. "Come on, get in. But . . . sorry. Your dog friend isn't invited."

The mutt watched forlornly as Kip climbed into the carriage. It was just an ordinary cab, but he'd never ridden in a carriage before. He worried about getting the leather seat dirty. Mrs. Brace gave him one of her warm smiles. "You're a regular Pied Piper, Kip. Animals and kids—they all warm up to you."

Rev. Brace had on his serious I've-got-an-idea look. "Kip, Mr. Smith has just returned by train from a trip to Michigan on behalf of the Children's Aid

Society. As we suspected, there are many good Christian families in the West willing to work with us placing some of our orphans—boys like Hooter, Ned, and Billy. The farmers can use a hand with some of the farm work, and the families Smith talked to are willing to treat such a boy as a member of the family. A few of our girls are also good candidates for placing out—I'm thinking of the Conner children and the Rogers girls."

Kip's mouth dropped open. "Davey? But . . . he's too small ta do any farm work. And Lauren and Lena—ain't they got parents somewhere?"

Mrs. Brace leaned over and laid a gloved hand on Kip's knee. "The future for homeless girls in New York is even worse than for the street rovers, Kip—you know that. Rev. Brace has asked up and down the docks for Mr. Conner, but the stepfather cannot be found. We'd like to find foster families for Davey and his sisters."

"And I have checked every lead for the Rogers girls' parents," said her husband. "The governess has totally disappeared, and no one who knew the Rogerses seems to know where the parents are or when they will return."

The carriage came to a stop in front of the Children's Aid Society, but Rev. Brace made no move to get out. "Mr. Smith thinks very highly of you, Kip. He told me about the broken knife you repaired—at your own initiative. He thinks you have a lot of potential to make something of your life, given an honest chance—and I agree." Rev. Brace leaned for-

ward. "What do you say? Are you willing to try a new life in the West?"

Kip pressed his back against the leather seat, his heart thudding in his chest. Excitement wrestled with fear in his mind. Of course he wanted to go west! What boy in his right mind wouldn't? But . . . he didn't know anything about the West. All he knew was how to survive on the streets—and barely that. What would it be like to have a family? What if no one wanted him? Or what if—?

Kip's old fear rose to the surface. "Ya wouldn't indenture me or the other rovers, would ya, Rev?"

Rev. Brace shook his head. "No, Kip. I promise. If it doesn't work out, one of our agents will come get you and bring you back home. But, Kip . . . one thing does trouble me." He held out his hand. "Will you empty your pockets, please?"

❖ ❖ ❖ ❖

Kip's ears still burned when he thought about emptying the corn out of his pocket into the Rev's outstretched hand. *"Kip, if you want to start a new life in the West,"* Rev. Brace had said, *"we have to get one thing straight—all thieving has got to stop. You can't just promise to do better. If you really mean it, you will make it right with Tibbs what you've been taking from him."*

But how could he make it right? If he told Mr. Tibbs that he'd been helping himself to his horse feed, Tibbs might just call the police! Or what if he said Kip owed him *all* the money Kip had been saving?

As Kip headed toward the newspaper drop-off the next morning, his fingers closed around the handful of paper money in his pocket. Paper money! At Rev. Brace's firm urging, Kip had asked Mr. Tracey to give him the money he'd been putting in the Lodging House "savings bank" over the past three months. But his mouth fell open when Mr. Tracey handed him six dollars! "Savings plus interest," Mr. Tracey said matter-of-factly. Six dollars! Kip had never felt so rich in his whole life!

But the closer he got to the newspaper drop-off, the slower he walked. A rover could live a long time on the street with six dollars! How easy it would be to lose himself among the tenements in the Five Points section again. He'd gotten along all right before Rev. Brace came along, hadn't he? And he wouldn't have to confess to Mr. Tibbs, either. He could do what he wanted, when he wanted, with no one snooping over his shoulder. . . .

He stopped. But if he didn't "make it right," the train going west would leave without him. Then what about his future?

Something butted him behind his knee. Looking down he saw the mutt that had tried to follow him the day before. The dog was old, and its ribs showed through its matted fur. Kip bent down and looked the dog in the eyes. "You and me . . . just a couple o' stray dogs, ain't we, pal." He straightened. "But me . . . I'm aimin' ta do somethin' about it!"

✧ ✧ ✧ ✧

"Mr. Tibbs just charged you a dollar for the feed and called it even?" Rev. Brace seemed surprised himself.

Kip grinned. "Yes, sir, Rev. Just looked at me funny-like when I told him I'd been nipping his horse feed and that I wanted ta make it right. Then he just wished me good luck on the orphan train."

An excited group of children from the Children's Aid Society swirled around Rev. and Mrs. Brace, Mr. Smith, and Mrs. Delaney on the deck of the *Isaac Newton*. The paddle-wheel riverboat would take them to Albany, New York, where they would catch the train west.

"The children look wonderful!" Mrs. Brace beamed from beneath her parasol. All the boys were scrubbed clean and dressed in new pants, shirts, and shoes. Peggy, Carlotta, Lauren, and Lena had crisp new dresses and hair bows. With a small nudge of pleasure, Kip noticed that Lena was clutching the carved rabbit he had made her.

"I look wonderful, too!" Davey Conner, clinging tightly to Kip's hand, hopped on one foot, then the other in his new jacket and short pants.

"*Especially* you." Mrs. Brace bent down and kissed the little boy.

The boat whistle blew. The girls put their hands over their ears and squealed. The boys playfully pushed each other and strutted up and down the deck.

Rev. Brace shook Kip's hand and winked. "Don't you worry about Pogo, now—I'll personally deliver him to Central Park, where he'll be in good company. . . . Mrs. Delaney! Mr. Smith! They're in your hands now. Godspeed!"

Rev. and Mrs. Brace hurried down the gangplank, then turned and waved at the excited children at the railing. The gangplank was pulled in, the ropes were cast off, and the big paddle wheel began churning.

As the *Isaac Newton* steamed into the Hudson River and turned north, Kip watched in wonder as the skyline of New York City sprawled on the starboard side. With a sudden impulse he snatched off his cap. "Three cheers for New York!"

At once nearly forty boys yanked off their caps and tossed them in the air. "Hip, hip, hooray!"

"An' three cheers for Michigan! Here we come!"

"Hip, hip, hooray!"

Chapter 8

Lost!

The starchy new clothes looked a little rumpled as the *Isaac Newton* pulled into the dock in Albany, New York, at six the next morning. The children were sleepy, but spirits were still high. The Conner and Rogers girls held hands in a line with Peggy at the head as they crossed the gangplank, while Kip held tightly to Davey's hand and tried to keep an eye on Hooter, Ned, and Billy so that no one would get lost in the unfamiliar surroundings.

With the practiced eye of a street rover, Kip noticed small heaps of ragged boys curled up together against large packing boxes along the docks or using a row of barrels as a shelter from the September wind off the river. Some were still sleeping, others stirring and staring in openmouthed wonder at the sight of a large crowd of children their own age unloading from the paddle-wheeler. The crowd on the dock swelled as other passengers got off the boat and pushed their way toward waiting cabs. The dock workers began slapping the boxes and barrels where the street children were sleeping. "Wake up! Get movin', ya little dock rats!"

Mr. Smith pulled out a train schedule, frowned, and pointed something out to Mrs. Delaney. Then he pulled out his pocket watch and squinted at it. He did not look happy.

"Boys! Boys and girls. Stay together so no one gets lost." Mr. Smith and Mrs. Delaney shepherded their flock of orphans out of the path of the main traffic on the docks. "Our train leaves at *noon*— that's six hours from now. We need to walk to—"

"Hey!" All the "dock rats" that had been sleeping on the docks were awake now, and some of the bigger ones circled the New Yorkers curiously. "What's a bunch o' sissies like y'all comin' ta Albany fer?" said the biggest boy. His clothes were little better than rags and his hair long and matted.

"Who ya callin' a bunch o' sissies?" snarled Hooter, balling up his fist.

"We can fight with the best o' ya!" shouted Ned.

The "dock rats" howled with laughter. "They *look* like a bunch o' swells, but they *sound* just like us!"

Kip's eyes and mouth tightened. Nobody in Five Points had ever laughed at him or his boys and gotten off easy. He was just about to join the word battle when he felt Lena tug on his sleeve. "Would you put Puffin in your pocket and keep him safe?" she whispered, holding out the little carved rabbit. Kip started to shake his head no, but Lena's eyes were round and scared.

Mr. Smith stepped forward. "Good morning, boys! These young people are on their way west to begin a new life . . . and we have a train to catch."

The "dock rats" parted, slouching and snickering. But as the orphan train riders fell into a line, two by two, the ragged onlookers fell into line behind them, hollering good-natured insults and mimicking their steps.

As the long line wound its way around the State Capitol building and down the street to the train depot, they attracted more of Albany's young street rovers. Mrs. Delaney walked tight-lipped beside the line, her dark eyes daring anyone to mess with her girls.

Kip walked steadily, keeping a good hold on Davey. But his eyes darted over the crowd. For just an instant he thought he saw a familiar face . . . but, no, that couldn't be possible. He didn't know anyone in Albany. His eyes searched again, but the face had disappeared.

At the train depot, the "orphan train riders" continued to be an object of curiosity to the ragged band of boys. "What ya want ta go all the way out West fer?"

"Why not?" the New York boys countered. "Ain't ya ever wanted ta see cowboys 'n Indians?"

"Come on, stay with us—ya'd like Albany."

"Better idea—why don't ya come with *us*?"

Mr. Smith hastily held up his hands. "Sorry, boys. Our party is full." He and Mrs. Delaney ushered their charges into the depot, filling it to overflowing. Other passengers stared and whispered behind their hands as the two agents tried to count the children to be sure they had everybody. Kip looked over the group, too . . . wait. Where was Hooter? And Ned and Billy?

A commotion at the door caught his attention. Hooter, Ned, and Billy rushed in noisily, dragging one of the local boys with them. "Look, Kip! Look what's here in Albany!"

Kip let go of Davey's hand and took several long strides forward. Under weeks of dirt and matted hair, the face *was* familiar. . . .

"Smack!" he yelled. "We thought ya was lost! How . . . ? What . . . ?" Kip could hardly keep from laughing out loud. "Are ya all right? Ya look a sight!"

Smack grinned through the streaked dirt on his face as Hooter, Ned, and Billy shoved each other and made a general fuss. Bit by bit Smack's story came out. He'd been hanging around the docks as usual, pestering the fish vendors, when a couple dock workers had grabbed him and put him on a boat going upriver. The crew had made him swab the deck and dump slop buckets, but he'd escaped when the boat got to Albany.

Then the grin faded and the dirty face looked at Kip forlornly. "Can I go with ya, Kip? I wanna get a new start out West, too."

Kip nodded. Of course! They couldn't just find Smack and then lose him again. He grabbed Smack

by the arm and dragged him over to Mr. Smith, spilling out the story. "He's gotta come with us, Mr. Smith. He's one of us. Can't you find a way?"

Mrs. Delaney stood to the side shaking her head. Mr. Smith frowned. "No decent farm family is going to take an orphan looking like that."

"We'll clean him up!" shouted Billy.

"I doubt it, but . . ." Mr. Smith gave up. "All right. Take him out to the horse trough and get him scrubbed. I'll see if we can get some clothes and a ticket."

With joyful hoots and hollers, Kip and his former band of rovers hustled Smack out to the horse trough, stripped off his rags, and dunked him in. Kip borrowed a curry brush from a dozing cabdriver and scrubbed a howling Smack till his skin was red. This was great entertainment to the Albany rovers, who cheered them on. Still soaking wet, Smack was dressed in a shirt and pair of long pants several sizes too large that looked suspiciously like Mr. Smith's "extra" clothes and marched back into the depot.

"That hair won't do," sniffed Mrs. Delaney. Smack's hair was still badly matted and full of knots. "A pair o' scissors—that's what we need."

A long whistle from a big black steam engine as the train puffed into the station drew a cheer from the restless children. Kip suddenly thought, *Davey!* But he saw that Peggy was pulling her little brother and Carlotta toward the train, so he shrugged and climbed on with the newly reformed Smack and the other boys.

Mr. Smith did his best to corral the New York orphans into the same car, but it was crowded and they ended up three or four to a seat. Everyone wanted to sit by the window. "Stay in your seats, everyone!" Mr. Smith kept urging. "Stay in your seats!"

Kip crowded into a seat with Smack and Billy.

Hooter and Ned sat in front of them with two other boys. Everyone squealed with excitement as the train jerked and, with a *shoosh, shoosh, shoosh*, pulled out of the depot.

Toward the front of the car, Kip caught a pensive little face looking at him over the back of a seat. Why was Lena looking at him like that? Then he remembered: her toy rabbit! With a stab of anxiety he felt in the pocket of his pants . . . *whew*! There it was. How easily it could have fallen out when he and the other boys were dunking Smack in the horse trough! Relieved, he made his way to the front of the car and handed the toy rabbit to the little girl. She rewarded him with a big smile and immediately began showing Puffin the sights out the window.

"Kip," said a pitiful voice, "can I come sit with you?" Davey was in the next seat with Peggy and Carlotta.

"Aw, Davey, we're kind of crowded back there." Kip was enjoying the freedom of not having the six-year-old tagging along. After all, he had a lot of catching up to do with Smack. "You've got a good seat up here . . . right, Peggy?" He looked at the older girl for support.

Peggy gave him a look—what kind of look was that?—and shrugged. "You can stay with me, Davey. Look! We're out in the country now!"

Relieved, Kip escaped to the back of the car and crowded in with Smack and Billy. The clatter of the wheels on the tracks and the creaks and groans of the train took them steadily away from the crowded brick and stone of the city, and green and gold fields began to rush past, dotted with cows and horses.

"What's that?" demanded Billy as they clattered past a field of golden spears.

"A cornfield, Billy," chuckled Mr. Smith from across the aisle.

"Oh yeah! Them's what makes buckwheaters!"

"Not buckwheat," said Kip. "Corn, ya know, like what I feed Pogo." Kip sighed and turned away. Pogo wouldn't be eating out of *his* hand anymore.

A farmer was plowing with a yoke of oxen. "Look at them cows!" said Hooter. "My gran'ma used ta milk cows back in the ol' country. . . . Well, I think so."

The September day was warm and golden. All the windows were down, raising the noise level and sending cinders and warm air rushing into the car.

"Oh! Oh! Oh! Look at them apples!" squealed Carlotta and Lena from the other side of the car. Heads and arms stretched out the windows as a grove of apple trees skimmed past. "Mr. Smith! Mr. Smith! Do they got apple trees in Michigan?"

More "ohhs" from the lively passengers. They were passing a field with big orange pumpkins dotting the ground. And again the question: "Do they got pumpkins in Michigan? What food we will eat when we get ta Michigan!"

Kip drank in the sight of green grass and trees, clusters of neat little farms, wide stretches of land without tenement buildings or sooty smoke. He saw a boy walking along a dirt road with a dog . . . not scrawny and old like the mutt back in New York who didn't have a home. But a bright-eyed dog with long black-and-white hair and a silky, wagging tail. Creamy brown cows lifted their heads and looked at the train as it passed. Horses spooked when the train blew its whistle, and galloped and bucked across the pasture.

An ache grew inside Kip like he was hungry. Not hungry for food, but hungry for . . . for what? He wasn't sure. But this was a world he hardly knew existed. Surely he would find . . . he would find his *future* there.

The afternoon wore on. Mrs. Delaney passed out apples, bread, and cheese. The train stopped here and there at little depots along the New York country-side, but no one was allowed to get off. Finally the train slowed—*shoosh, shoosh, shooooooooosh*—and pulled off on a siding to take on water and firewood.

Mr. Smith clapped his hands. "All right, children, we'll be here for an hour. You can all get out and stretch your legs, or get a drink of water in the barrels by the depot, but don't get out of sight of the train! We don't want to leave anyone behind." Eagerly all the children scrambled off and raced down the siding to the water barrels. The first one was empty but the other one had a dipper, which the children all passed around. Mrs. Delaney marched off with Peggy and Lauren to find some milk for the children, and Mr. Smith took a somewhat reluctant Smack by the arm to see if he could find a pair of barber scissors. Kip, Hooter, Ned, and Billy followed along, enjoying Smack's discomfort.

All too soon the train whistle blew two short toots, the signal to return to the train. The boys laughed and pointed at the embarrassed Smack, whose matted hair had been clipped down to mere stubble. "It'll grow, it'll grow," said Mr. Smith as he boosted the smaller children up into the train. As the children settled into their seats, Mr. Smith started counting heads. "Is everybody here?"

Outside they heard the conductor give the call: "All aboooooard!"

"Wait! Davey . . . where's Davey?" Peggy Conner leaped up from her seat and started back down the aisle, anxiously looking left and right.

"Aw, he's probably just playin' hide-and-seek," said Kip. Half a dozen heads ducked to check under the seats. No Davey. Mr. Smith quickly swung off the train and frantically waved both arms at the conductor, who was just about to give the "All clear" signal to the engineer.

Quickly the conductor and Mr. Smith checked all the other passenger cars, while an anxious Peggy and the other children hung out the windows. His own worry mounting, Kip also got off and did a quick check of the depot and looked up and down both sides of the tracks.

Five minutes . . . ten . . . fifteen went by. Finally Kip, the conductor, and Mr. Smith all returned to the train car empty-handed.

Little Davey Conner was lost.

Chapter 9

The Matching Game

Peggy and Carlotta spilled off the train. "Oh, Mr. Smith! Don't let the train go. We have ta find Davey!"

"Don't worry, Peggy. We won't leave . . . but think! When was the last time you saw him? Where do you think he might be?"

Guilt nagged at the corners of Kip's conscience. He should have been keeping an eye on the little kid. But he quickly brushed those thoughts away. Peggy was Davey's older sister, wasn't she? Why should he have to look out for Davey all the time—especially on the train, where all the boys and girls were together?

Peggy hugged herself as she paced back and forth. "He . . . he was upset because Kip and the other boys went off without him. . . . So I just told him to stay in the car. That's the last time I saw him!"

Mr. Smith scratched his head. "Well, he has to be around here somewhere, unless . . ." Mr. Smith looked down the track into the distance. Kip gulped. The unspoken words hung in the air. Had Davey wandered off down the track, not knowing the danger? Or had a passing stranger lured him away?

Peggy suddenly grabbed Kip's arm. "I don't think Davey's lost. I think he's *hiding. You* have ta find him, Kip. He'll listen ta you. Please!"

Kip scowled. "Hiding! What do ya mean?"

Peggy gripped his arm harder. "He thought ya didn't care 'bout him anymore. Go on—holler fer him. He'll come to you."

"Worth a try, son," said Mr. Smith. "We'll keep looking, too—but you do the calling, all right?"

Frustrated, Kip looked up and down the track. Why was Peggy trying to make Davey's disappearance his fault? Still, the little boy *was* missing. "Davey!" he yelled. "Where are ya, Davey?" He went back inside the empty depot. "Davey, are ya in here? Davey!" The stationmaster just shook his head. Kip went outside and circled the depot. He took a quick drink from the water barrel as he passed, then continued his search.

What was he supposed to do? Mr. Smith and the conductor had already checked all the train cars. He saw the conductor looking beneath the train cars, and Mr. Smith talking to some workmen at the water tower that had refilled the train.

If Davey was just hiding, why wasn't he answering? Maybe he really was lost. But if he *was* hiding ... Kip's mind began to spark. If *he* were Davey, where would he hide?

Kip tried to put himself in the little boy's shoes. If he wanted to hide, he wouldn't hide in sight of the train. Too easy to be found by just anyone. But if he wanted to be found eventually, he wouldn't run far away. Let's see ... he'd hide ... Kip turned slowly around looking at the water tower, the train cars, the depot, the water barrels ...

The water barrels! Kip walked quickly to the side of the depot, his anger rising. He had just walked past those water barrels, calling Davey's name. If Davey was hiding in an empty one and hadn't answered him ...

Kip removed the loose-fitting cover to the empty water barrel and peered inside. The barrel was dark, and it took a moment or two for his eyes to adjust. But there in the bottom of the barrel was Davey Conner, sound asleep.

❖ ❖ ❖

The westward train chugged into the night, heading for Buffalo. The oil lamps were turned low, and the exhausted children slept, leaning against one another in the wicker seats. Kip watched the sleeping Davey, squished happily between himself and Billy.

"What'd ya go an' scare us fer, Davey?" Kip had demanded as he'd tipped the barrel over and pulled out the little boy.

Startled awake, Davey had stuck out his lip. *"I hate Smack! Ya used ta be my friend till he came back."*

Kip had picked him up and brushed off the damp dirt clinging to his new clothes. *"Nah, ya got it all wrong, Davey. I'm happy to see Smack, true enough . . . but I'll always be yer big brother, okay?"*

The little boy had wrapped his arms and legs tightly around Kip as Kip had carried him back to the train.

Peggy and Carlotta were beside themselves with joy. Even Lena shyly came forward and handed Davey her carved rabbit. *"You can play with Puffin for a while, Davey. He'll make you feel better."*

But as the train continued westward, Kip had an uneasy feeling. He had no idea what was going to happen when they got to Michigan. Had he just made a promise he couldn't keep?

✧ ✧ ✧ ✧

When the *Michigan Central* finally pulled into Dowagiac, Michigan, at three in the morning, the little band of orphans was wide-eyed and silent. The trip had taken four days, including a nine-hour lay-over in Buffalo, New York, during which Mrs. Delaney had been worn to a frazzle trying to keep track of over forty orphans. Then a long, rough lake passage from Buffalo to Detroit by another steamship, during which half the children got seasick.

On the final leg of the journey from Detroit to Dowagiac by train, the children were alternately laughing in delight at the sights along the way and staring soberly into space. Similar thoughts wove tangled webs in their heads: *Will somebody want me? Will I like my new family? Will I ever see my friends again? What do people* do *in the country?*

The stationmaster's jaw dropped when Mr. Smith and Mrs. Delaney shepherded their sleepy flock into the depot. "Oh my, oh my. You're the . . . of course! From the Children's Aid Society. But . . . there's nobody to meet you this hour of the night!"

"That's all right. We understand." Mr. Smith looked wearily around the tiny waiting room. "Can we just wait here till morning?"

"Wait here? Oh my." The stationmaster just shook his head and disappeared into a back room as the children spread out on the floor to doze until morning.

Kip was one of the first to awaken. On his way out the door to use the privy behind the depot, he saw a flyer posted on the depot door. Kip sounded out the words: *"WANTED—HOMES FOR CHILDREN."* There were a lot of other words in smaller letters he couldn't read. But that paper must be talking about them!

By the time he got back, all the children were yawning and stretching and heading for the privies. "Are we *really* in Michigan?" Hooter wanted to know. When the answer was yes, nearly every boy and girl scattered outside to explore.

Kip hung back. A question had been nagging him. "Um, Mr. Smith. What if . . . how do we know a family is going to take us?"

Mr. Smith smiled encouragingly. "Don't worry about it, son. As big and strong as you are? There will be farm families fighting over you. Now, go on. I'm going to go rustle us up some breakfast!"

By the time Mr. Smith got back from the local hotel carrying a pail of milk and a large basket of sliced ham, cold biscuits, and jam, the boys were straggling back loaded down with evidence that they had indeed arrived in the new Promised Land.

"Look! Apples! Just hangin' on a tree!" cried Billy and Ned, holding out their caps.

"I found me some pumpkin skin, just thrown away—can ya believe it?"

And so it went. Pockets, caps, shirt sleeves, and skirts were filled with cornhusks, acorns, even peaches that had fallen on the ground. Lena and Carlotta each handed Mrs. Delaney and Mr. Smith a bunch of wild flowers. "They were growing right on the *road*!"

Just then the stationmaster bustled out from behind his window. "No, no. You can't bring that dog in here! Besides, he belongs to the judge! Shoo! Shoo! Go home!"

The boys burst out laughing as a small yellow dog dodged the stationmaster and peered out from between Kip's legs, panting happily. Kip pretended to look surprised. "Must've follered me in. I think he smelled breakfast."

The dog was chased outside and the breakfast eagerly consumed. Then Mr. Smith said, "Do you know what day this is?"

"Christmas?" Davey asked hopefully.

Mr. Smith smiled. "No, it's Sunday, the Lord's Day. To start this very special day when you will be meeting your new parents, we are going to church!"

❖ ❖ ❖ ❖

Once again the "orphan train riders" made quite a parade as they walked down the streets of Dowagiac to the Presbyterian church, which met in the schoolhouse. It was hard to know who did more staring— the townspeople and country folk, gaping at the little band in their rumpled clothes marching two by two into the church, or the homeless children, as they eyed the buggies and wagons pulling up to the schoolhouse.

Smack poked Kip. "My eyes, look at that pair o' big horses—purty as you please. I'd go fer *that* farmer takin' me in."

"Yeah, but *that* one gots a roof on his carriage," Billy said. "I'll bet he's *rich*."

Davey tugged on Kip's sleeve. "Lookee, Kip. That woman in the straw hat don't have no children. I bet she needs a little boy."

Kip said nothing. His palms were sweaty, and he could feel his heart beating. Today was the day! *Soon, very soon . . .*

The forty-six children and two Society agents took up a good deal of the space in the schoolhouse-turned-church. But the first song was one Rev. Brace had taught the boys in Boys' Meetings, so they joined right in. Heads nodded in approval. The next hymn Kip didn't know, but he hummed along and tapped his foot. Happiness pushed a smile onto his face. *Soon, very soon . . .*

The preacher didn't tell Bible stories as well as Rev. Brace, and the children got restless. But the Presbyterian pastor wisely cut the service short and introduced their guests. "Mr. Smith, please tell us about the Children's Aid Society and your purpose in bringing these children to our town."

Every face was spellbound as Mr. Smith described the condition of homeless children on the streets of New York. "Some people would simply house these children in orphanages or asylums. But institutional life destroys initiative and hope, the very virtues that make this country great! Institutions keep the body alive but allow the soul to rot, creating a hope-less class easily sucked into crime and vice. It is the intent of the Children's Aid Society to place as many of these bright children as we can with good Christian families here in the West. The benefit is three-fold: Farm families like yourselves gain another pair of willing hands; the children receive the benefit of loving families and parental attention; and we re-duce the criminal class of the future from our east-ern cities by turning these youngsters into productive citizens."

The congregation clapped long and loud, and then the service ended. Baskets were pulled out of wagons and buggies as families spread out picnics in the school yard. Food was shared with the orphans, who did a good job of looking hungry. Soon other wagons began arriving, and the whole assembly gathered back inside the schoolhouse. This time the forty-six children with their clean faces and travel-worn clothing were seated on rows of benches facing the curious onlookers.

Kip searched each face that came in. *Soon, very soon . . .*

Each of the children was asked to stand and say his or her name. A stout fellow with white whiskers and a black suit kept asking, "And what is *your* story, young man?" or "young miss?" When Lauren and Lena said their parents had "gone missing," and

their governess didn't want to take care of them anymore, mouths dropped in shock. Davey hung his head and said, "Mama died, and then it was only Peggy and Carlotta and me." Several women pulled out handkerchiefs and dabbed at their eyes.

When it was Kip's turn, the man asked, "How did *you* end up at the Children's Aid Society, young man—Kip, is it?"

Kip swallowed. *Soon, very soon* . . . "Yes, sir, Kip O'Reilly, sir. Uh . . . Rev. Brace came to the jail, sir, and got me out if I would come to the Boys' Lodging House and stay off the—"

"*Jail*, did you say, young man?" The white-whiskered face became a dark cloud. "And what, pray tell, were you in jail *for*?"

Kip was startled. He looked at Mr. Smith. What should he do? Mr. Smith looked worried, but he gave

a slow nod. Kip must tell the truth.

Kip swallowed again. "Fer thievin', sir, but I ain't been—"

"Thieving!" the man bellowed. "That is what I was afraid of!—young thieves being fostered upon us in the disguise of innocent children. The Children's Aid Society plays upon our sympathies, oh yes. But Mr. Smith said it himself—they want to rid the New York streets of the future criminal class. Well, we do not want their criminals *here*!"

There was a stunned silence. Then whispers and murmurs spread like water through the schoolhouse. Kip wanted to turn and run, but he stumbled backward and sat down.

The Presbyterian pastor held up his hands. "Ladies! Gentlemen! Quiet, please . . . Judge, I'm sure your concern is well noted. But I have read the literature written by the good Rev. Brace and talked with Mr. Smith several times. True, these children come from hard circumstances. But the Children's Aid Society has selected the most promising children for this journey, children who deserve a chance. They will also follow up with every child to be sure a good match is made. My good people, let us do our Christian duty and open our homes to those less fortunate than ourselves."

With the pastor's encouragement, the last introductions of the children were made. Then Mr. Smith was given a small table, and interested couples pushed forward with letters of recommendation from their pastor or other town dignitaries. The families were encouraged to talk personally to the children, and when they made their selection, to bring the child to the table to sign the necessary papers of agreement.

As Mr. Smith predicted, the bigger boys were some of the first to go. "Hey, Kip, lookee here!" Hooter shouted. "I got myself a family! Man says I can learn ta plow!" Even Smack, with his bare feet and clipped head, was soon shaking hands with an older man in farmer's overalls.

Kip tried to smile and wave good-bye to his friends, but his mouth was dry. Not a single family so far had stopped to talk to him.

He saw a pleasant-looking couple with several small boys talking to Peggy. Peggy motioned hopefully to Carlotta and Davey, too, but the couple shook their head. Kip stared. Weren't the families going to take brothers and sisters together?

But Davey was doing his own searching. He made a beeline for the woman in the straw bonnet who was still sitting on the benches and crawled right up in her lap. "I'd like to be *your* little boy, ma'am." And he threw his arms around her neck.

"Oh, Emmet," the woman said to her husband, who looked quite taken aback. "We just have to take him home with us."

A well-dressed couple that looked like they lived in town came up to the table holding Lauren and Lena by the hand. "We only intended to adopt one girl," the woman confessed to Mr. Smith, "but we just can't separate these sweet sisters!" Lauren and

Lena were clinging to each other in happy relief.

More and more wagons pulled into the school yard with families from surrounding towns, even as wagons with their new foster children headed for home. The process took all afternoon, but finally the last wagon had pulled out of the school yard, and every child had been spoken for. . . .

Except Kip.

Chapter 10

A Second Chance

Kip just stared at the ground as he and Mr. Smith walked slowly back to the train depot. He felt like slugging something, but instead thrust his hands into his pockets.

Mr. Smith rested an arm on Kip's shoulder. "I'm so sorry, Kip."

Kip jerked away. "It ain't fair! Most all the other rovers did thievin' at one time or other. Only way ta live sometimes."

"I know that. I—"

Kip exploded. "Why didn't ya tell that ta the judge, then?" He broke into a run, leaving Mr. Smith in his wake.

At the depot he flopped onto a bench, his chest heaving. As his breathing slowed, so did his thoughts. He knew why Mr. Smith didn't announce that most of the other street rovers had been petty thieves, too. The judge would've turned the town against the whole lot of them, and then none of the boys would've gotten families. If only he hadn't mentioned that Rev. Brace got him out of the jail!

Mr. Smith finally arrived at the depot platform and sat down beside Kip. "Kip, both Rev. Brace and I believe you deserve a chance. Making things right with Mr. Tibbs took courage, showed character. Now, Mrs. Delaney is going back to New York on the next train. You *could* go with her. But . . . I was planning to go on to a few other towns and arrange for the next orphan train—you could come with me. I'm sure in another town we could find a farm family eager to have you. What happened today was unfortunate— but that doesn't mean it would happen again."

Kip kept his face turned away from Mr. Smith, staring without seeing the town of Dowagiac sprawled to the left and right. He didn't want to go to another town. All his friends, the closest to a family he'd ever had—Hooter and Smack and Ned and Billy, little Davey and Peggy and Carlotta, and Lauren and Lena—had been placed *here*.

But the same was true if he went back to New York. What "future" did he have back there?

Kip shook his head in despair. He didn't know what to do.

"That's all right, you think about it for a while," said Mr. Smith, rising. "I'm going to check train schedules and talk to Mrs. Delaney. She's over at the hotel resting. I'll come back for you in a while." Mr. Smith went into the depot, then a short time later came out and walked down the street to the small hotel.

Kip watched him go, his mind blank. He didn't know what to do. The bench was the only solid thing in his life right then.

Time seemed to stand still. A fly buzzed in his ear, then flew away. A farm horse plodded along the dusty street, pulling a wagon. The late-September sun was setting, streaking the sky with pink and yellow clouds. Funny. He hardly ever saw the sky in New York. Too many buildings crowded together—

"Hello."

Kip jumped. A little girl wearing a Sunday dress and bonnet was standing right beside the bench he sat on. Lacy pantalettes showed beneath her dress. She looked about Lena's age, maybe eight.

"Why are you sitting here all by yourself?" The little girl's brown eyes looked at him curiously. Dark hair peeked out beneath her straw bonnet. "Did you come on the orphan train?"

Nosy kid. But Kip nodded.

"Aren't you going to stay?"

Kip shook his head.

"But don't you want a family?"

Kip swallowed an angry retort. The little girl didn't mean any harm. But he wished she would go away. "Where's yer mama, little girl? Shouldn't be off by yerself—gonna be night soon."

"Oh, she's coming." The little girl continued to

stare at him. "She took some soup to old Mrs. Bracken. She's been sick." She turned and pointed to a small house across the street. "Over there."

Just then a woman came out of the little house and looked around. "Nell? Nell!" They could hear her calling. "Where are you? Come on, now, we're ready to go."

Kip watched as the little girl ran across the street, grabbed her mother's gloved hand, and pulled her back to the train depot. "Mama, mama! This boy came on the orphan train, and nobody took him home! Can we take him home, please, Mama?"

Kip felt his cheeks turn hot. He pulled off his cap and stood awkwardly to his feet. "I . . . I'm sorry, ma'am. Don't know where she got such an idea."

The woman looked puzzled. "Is that true? You came on the orphan train?"

Kip nodded. Out of the corner of his eye he saw Mr. Smith come out of the hotel and start toward the depot. Help was on the way.

"Please, Mama. Let's take him home. Otherwise he'll have to sleep right here on that bench till the train comes."

"Oh my. Well, I don't know . . ."

Mr. Smith stepped onto the platform and tipped his hat. "Good evening, ma'am. I'm Mr. Smith, agent for the Children's Aid Society of New York. Don't think I've had the pleasure, Mrs. . . . ?"

The woman held out her gloved hand. "Mrs. Donaldson, and this is my daughter, Nell. My husband is the veterinarian here in Dowagiac. We live right on the edge of town. Are you—? Is this—? I mean, what will happen with this boy?"

Veterinarian? Kip had never heard that word. What did a "veterinarian" do?

Mr. Smith pursed his lips a moment and looked at Kip. Then, "That is yet to be decided. I am catching a train tomorrow to visit towns in Indiana and Illinois. I will continue looking for a home for him."

"Oh my." The woman paced three steps this way, then three steps back, as if thinking to herself. "We knew the orphan train was coming, of course. Everyone was talking about it. But my husband is a very busy man—he's the only vet for miles around. Always going out to this farm or that. Always some emergency when it comes to animals, you know!" She laughed nervously. "But it seems a shame for this boy not to know hospitality in our town even for one night."

Kip's curiosity got the better of him. "Say, what's a veter . . . um, vet'in . . ."

Mrs. Donaldson smiled. She had the same dark hair and warm brown eyes as Nell. "Veterinarian. My husband's a doctor for animals—when they get hurt or sick."

Kip's eyes rounded. He had never heard of such a thing.

The woman seemed to make up her mind. "Mr. Smith, we would be happy to take this young man home for the night, give him a home-cooked supper and a bed before you continue your journey." She turned to Kip. "Would you like that . . . what is your name?"

"Kip O'Reilly, ma'am." Kip felt awkward, but he

sure would like to meet a man who doctored sick animals. "Yes, ma'am. I'd like that fine."

Mr. Smith's eyebrows went up. "Well, then. I will come by your home tomorrow noon to pick him up. Our train is at three."

❖ ❖ ❖

Kip had never seen such a meal as Mrs. Donaldson put on the table that night. Thick chicken stew with carrots and potatoes, warm biscuits, butter and jam, applesauce, and peach cobbler. Kip grabbed a biscuit right off, but Mrs. Donaldson said, "Let's give thanks first."

Embarrassed, Kip bowed his head. Rev. Brace prayed at the Boys' Meetings, and Mr. Tracey said "grace" at the Lodging House supper. But he didn't know regular people prayed. He snuck a look at Mrs. Donaldson. "And, Lord, thank you for our guest this evening. We ask that you will give him a good home and a future. Amen."

Kip was halfway through his third biscuit when he heard a horse and buggy drive into the yard. Nell jumped up and peeked between the curtains. "Daddy's back!" Ten minutes later, Dr. Donaldson came into the kitchen through the back door wearing boots, work pants, and a rumpled coat. He shot a questioning look at his wife when he saw Kip.

Mrs. Donaldson hurriedly dished up a plate full of chicken stew and biscuits as she attempted to explain Kip's presence. Kip squirmed under the man's probing gaze. Finally Dr. Donaldson pushed his plate away and wiped his mouth with his napkin. "Well, now. The good Lord tells us to be hospitable. So you can stay the night. But any young man under my roof had better be up early to help with chores. Woodbox needs filling." He turned to his wife. "I've got to go back out to the Pattersons in the morning to check on the cow. May need to pop that stomach."

Questions leaped into Kip's mind. What was wrong with the cow? What was Dr. Donaldson going to do? But he said nothing. What was the use? He was leaving Dowagiac the next day anyway.

But the same questions rolled over in his mind as he tried to go to sleep a while later in a small room upstairs under the eaves. The comforter was warm. The pillow was soft and smelled like sunshine. But he almost felt too excited to sleep. But why? He was only going to stay here one night.

Kip woke with a start. Fingers of light tickled the wall opposite the one small window, but it wasn't full daylight. He listened, but heard no sounds in the house. Pulling on his pants and shoes, he crept down the narrow staircase and into the kitchen. The woodbox beside the cookstove had only one stick of wood. He was supposed to "fill the woodbox," but how?

Quietly he opened the back door. By a lean-to he saw a huge stack of sawed-off logs. Easy enough. He'd carry a few inside. But when he came back in with a log, he realized there was no way it would fit inside the round openings on the top of the stove, not even in the square door of the oven. He took the log

back outside. An ax was sticking out of a big log standing on its end by the woodpile. Maybe he was supposed to split them.

The sun was up and sweat was pouring down

Kip's back by the time he got the first log split into four pieces. Time and time again he had swung the ax and missed. But finally, by trial and error, he split three logs. As he gathered up the pieces and started for the house, he realized Dr. Donaldson was standing in the doorway, eating an apple and watching him. He stepped aside as Kip dumped his load of wood into the box, then grabbed his hat from its peg. "Want to ride along to the Pattersons?"

Kip looked around. Was Dr. Donaldson talking to *him*? "Uh . . . yes, sir!"

"Grab an apple from the bowl and come on, then."

Within a short time, Dr. Donaldson had led a trim gray horse out of the barn, hitched it to an open carriage, and set off down the road, heading away from town. Trees and split-rail fences seemed to fly by in the lush countryside. Kip tried not to think about the decision he must make within a few hours: back to New York, or take his chances in another town.

Dr. Donaldson pulled lightly on the reins in his right hand, and the horse turned smoothly into a lane, past a modest farmhouse, and pulled up beside the big weather-beaten barn. Kip hopped out and waited as Dr. Donaldson went around to the back of the carriage and unloaded a black bag and a couple pairs of heavy gloves, then a long piece of rubber hose and a short length of metal pipe, which he handed to Kip to carry.

Inside the barn, Kip smelled sweet hay and the pungent smell of manure. The tails of several cows poked out from a row of milking stalls. A man's head

with a crumpled felt hat poked up between the stalls.
" 'Lo, Doc. Thanks for coming back. Dolly's not much
better—still all blown up." The man peered through
the dim light. "See you got a helper this morning."

"Yep." Dr. Donaldson headed for a back stall. Kip
followed. Mr. Patterson looked vaguely familiar . . .
where had Kip seen him before? But he didn't have
time to think about it. A sweet-faced Jersey cow
stood with hanging head, her belly blown up like a
balloon. Working quickly, Dr. Donaldson tied the
cow's front legs together, then hind legs. While Mr.
Patterson and Kip pulled on the hind legs, the vet
pulled on the front and soon the cow went down with
a long moan.

"Come up here and hold this rope, Kip. Don't let
her kick." Kip held tightly to the rope at the cow's
front end, watching in fascination as the vet pried
open the cow's mouth and inserted the short metal
pipe. Then he began threading the rubber hose
through the pipe and down her throat.

Kip was sure the cow would choke to death on
that hose! But all Dr. Donaldson said was, "Stand
back, Kip. She's gonna—"

Aaauuuuuugggggghhhh! A blast of putrid air burst
from the hose with a long, guttural burp. The stink
made Kip's stomach lurch. But Dr. Donaldson was
quickly pulling out the hose and removing the pipe.
"Let her up!" Kip darted in and loosed the rope from the
cow's front legs. Mr. Patterson loosed the rear legs. In a
moment Dolly had scrambled to her feet, her creamy
brown sides softly rounded and normal looking.

"Now, ain't that something," chuckled Mr. Patterson.

"Better milk her before she gets too uncomfortable." Dr. Donaldson picked up his bag and motioned for Kip to get the slimy pipe and hose. He was glad for the gloves.

"My eyes! I never saw nothin' like that before!" Kip was grinning from ear to ear. "Only critter I ever helped was a pigeon with a broken wing."

Dr. Donaldson looked at him sideways. "You helped a wounded pigeon?"

"Yep. Named him Pogo. Became fond o' me. Had ta leave him behind, though—when I came on the orphan train, I mean." Kip's voice dropped. He'd almost forgotten he had to catch a train today—back to New York or . . . where, he didn't know.

Had he said something wrong? Dr. Donaldson was looking at him kind of funny. But all he said was, "Put that stuff away, will you, Kip? I've got to see Patterson a minute."

Kip grabbed a rag from the back of the carriage and wiped the hose and pipe before putting them away. As he waited, he heard childish laughter coming from the grassy yard beside the house. Several young children were taking turns on a swing hanging from a tall branch. An older girl was pushing one of the children high, while another danced impatiently by her side. "My turn! My turn! Now push *me*, Peggy!"

Kip stared. The girl pushing the children was Peggy Conner!

Chapter 11

Broken Dreams

Peggy!" Kip was so glad to see Peggy he could hardly run to the yard fast enough. So that's where he had seen Mr. Patterson—the Pattersons had chosen Peggy to go home with them!

"Kip?" Peggy's eyes were wide. "What are *you* doing here? Mrs. P said the vet . . . oh, Kip! Did ya get adopted after all? I thought—"

Kip shrugged casually. "Naw. The Donaldsons just took me in fer the night. Mr. Smith is comin' fer me today. But . . . at least I got ta see ya again. Is it good here?"

"I guess so. I think they need help with all these little boys, but . . . Mrs. P is nice. Likes having a girl ta talk ta,

I think. Mr. P is all right, too. Said I can start school in town next week. I just wish . . ." Peggy's chin trembled.

"I know. Ya wish ya could be with Davey and Carlotta." Kip grabbed Peggy's arm. "But think on it this way—at least ya all got placed in the same town. Yer gonna see each other, know how they're doin'."

If only Peggy knew how lucky she really was.

"Kip! Let's go!" Mr. Donaldson was climbing into the buggy.

"Bye, Peggy. If ya see Davey—or Hooter or any o' the rest o' my rovers—tell 'em I'll never fergit any o' ya!" With a last wave, Kip ran to the buggy and climbed in. He turned back and watched till the Patterson farm dipped out of sight.

Mr. Donaldson was quiet on the way home, and Kip was just as glad. Part of him was glad he'd seen Peggy, could imagine where she was living now . . . but part of him wished he hadn't. Made it harder knowing he was leaving and would never see her again.

Mr. Smith was already at the Donaldson home sharing a cup of coffee with Mrs. Donaldson when Kip and Mr. Donaldson walked in the back door. Kip looked around for Nell—she must be off to school. The Children's Aid Society agent smiled. "Looks like you've had a full morning, Kip. But . . . we better be getting back to town. Mrs. Delaney is waiting for us at the depot."

"Uh, I've been thinking. . . ." Mr. Donaldson cleared his throat. "Haven't had a chance to talk to my wife yet, but . . . Kip here seems to have a liking for working with animals—did a good job this morning. Maybe we could take him on, give it a try."

Kip's heart lurched. Would the Donaldsons *really* take him in? He had hardly dared to think about the possibility, but now that the words had been spoken, Kip realized he had never wanted anything so badly in his whole life.

He looked at Mr. Smith and saw concern in his eyes. And Kip knew. Knew that half the town heard the judge declare he wasn't wanted here. "That would be wonderful, Mr. and Mrs. Donaldson," Smith said gravely. "But there is one thing—"

"You mean about Kip being in jail?" Mr. Donaldson looked at his wife. "Patterson told me—told me about the judge making a big fuss, and no one taking the boy after that. But Patterson saw the boy work this morning. Agrees with me. Thinks we ought to give the boy a chance."

Kip felt weak in the knees. He couldn't speak. But when Mrs. Donaldson moved to his side and gave him a warm hug, he hugged her back. Was it possible? Really possible that he had a future?

✧ ✧ ✧ ✧

Kip swung the ax—hard—and the log split in two with the first swing.

The back door banged. "Bravo!" said a familiar voice, laughing.

Kip looked up. "Mr. Smith! You back already?"

Mr. Smith had said he'd stop in Dowagiac in a couple weeks on his way back to New York and see how each of the children was doing. Kip looked at him sideways. "Ya ain't gonna take me back, are ya?"

Mr. Smith grinned and shook his head. "I've just been talking to the Donaldsons. Mr. Donaldson says he hasn't had to fill the woodbox once since you've been here." He winked at Kip. "Don't think he misses swinging that ax." The agent pulled out his handkerchief and mopped his head. "Sure is warm for October! How about you, Kip? Things going all right?"

"Better'n all right, Mr. Smith. Mrs. Donaldson signed me up at the school—same place we had church, remember?—and guess who's there? *All* the rovers and other orphans—even Davey is goin' ta first grade! So I get ta see all my friends near every day." Kip grinned. "An' when I'm not in school, Mr. Donaldson lets me go with him when he does his animal doctorin'. Yesterday he saved the judge's dog what ate rat poison. I say! That was one mighty sick dog. Say, Mr. Smith . . ." Kip lowered his voice. "Do ya think I could be a vet'inary like him someday?"

"Don't see why not, young man. You've got a good head on your shoulders. If you study hard, no reason you couldn't go to college."

Kip blinked. "C-college? Ain't it just like farmin'—watchin' and learnin'?"

Mr. Smith laughed. "Better talk to Mr. Donaldson. He knows better than I do."

❖ ❖ ❖ ❖

Michigan's warm October faded to a crisp November. Only a few leaves still clung to their trees. Most of the bare trees looked like the bristles on the currycomb Kip used to groom Mr. Donaldson's gray mare.

He was giving Misty, the horse, one last brush over her sleek hide one Saturday morning when Nell came running to the barn. "Kip! Mama wants you to go to the post office. Can I go with you?" The little girl clutched her arms and hopped up and down.

"What are ya doin' out here without a coat, Nell Donaldson?" Kip hung up the currycomb, shooed Nell out of the barn, and latched the door. As he hustled the little girl back into the warm kitchen, Kip frowned. Mr. Donaldson often took him on vet calls on the weekend—but he might miss the chance if he was in town at the post office. He could hurry, but if Nell went with him . . .

Mrs. Donaldson was down on her knees cutting remnants of cloth with a huge pair of scissors. "Kip, would you take those letters to the General Store? And please take Nell with you. I need to work on these costumes for the Christmas pageant with no interruptions."

Kip took the letters from the table, then hesitated. "Uh . . . tell Mr. Donaldson I'll be right back . . . if he has ta make calls today, I mean."

Mrs. Donaldson nodded absently and continued cutting.

Kip waited impatiently while Nell put on her coat and hat, then took her hand and walked briskly down the road into town. The Donaldsons lived on the far edge of town, and it took twenty minutes to walk to Compton's General Store, which also served as Dowagiac's post office. Thirty minutes today, since he had to slow down for Nell.

"Mornin', Mr. Compton," he said, pushing open the door of the dry goods store. A bell tinkled overhead. "Davey anywhere abou—uhhhh." Kip's words were cut off as his legs were tackled from behind. Davey giggled in delight as Kip grabbed the little boy, turning him upside down. "Davey Conner, you're faster than a greased pig. . . . Here, Nell, give these letters to Mr. Compton."

Errand done. Now they could get back home—if Davey would let go.

"Oh, Kip." Mr. Compton came out from behind his counter. "Letter came yesterday for the Stewarts— from Rev. Brace at the Children's Aid Society." Kip's ears pricked. The Stewarts were Lauren and Lena's foster family here in town. "But don't know if they'll come in today and maybe it's something important. Would you take it over to them?"

Kip felt torn. He wanted to get home in case Mr. Donaldson went out on any calls . . . but a letter from Rev. Brace for the Stewarts? What could it be?

"All right. Nell, ya stay here an' play with Davey, okay? I'll be right back."

"I want to play with Lena!" Nell stamped her foot.

Kip was already out the door. "Another time! We can't stay today!" He ran down the main street, turned down a side street, then another, and stopped in front of a pleasant frame house with orange and yellow mums still blooming in the flower bed.

Lauren answered his knock. Her face lit up and she grabbed his hand, pulling him into the sitting room. "Mama Stewart! It's Kip!"

Mrs. Stewart was reading, her rich auburn hair parted in the middle and swept into a coiled knot at the back of her head. Kip pulled off his cap. "Morning, Mrs. Stewart. Mr. Compton wanted me ta bring this letter ta ya." Kip glanced around curiously.

"If you're looking for Lena, she's outside playing with her pet rabbit." Mrs. Stewart shook her head. "I honestly don't know what got into us! A rabbit!" She laughed ruefully as she took the letter. "Hmm. From Rev. Brace at the Children's Aid Society . . ." She loosened the seal, unfolded the page, and started to read. A few moments later she let out a startled cry.

"Mama?" Lauren rushed to her side.

Mrs. Stewart looked up, her face ashen. "It's . . . it's your mother, Lauren. Mrs. Rogers appeared at the Children's Aid Society and is demanding that Rev. Brace return you to New York as soon as possible!"

❖ ❖ ❖ ❖

Kip collected Nell from Compton's General Store and walked quickly back toward the Donaldson place. "Kip!" Nell whined. "Don't walk so fast."

But Kip didn't answer. He kept thinking about Rev. Brace's letter. Lauren had only stared at hearing the news that her real mother had shown up, as if she couldn't speak. But when Lena heard the news, she had balled up her fists and yelled, "No! I don't want to go back! *You're* my mother now!" And the little girl had run up the stairs and slammed the door to the girls' room.

Kip didn't know what to think. Back in New York he had kept expecting Mr. and Mrs. Rogers to show up. But not since they'd come all the way out west on the orphan train, and Lauren and Lena had found a new home. How would he feel if his real mother and father wanted him back? He shook the thought out of his head. Couldn't happen. His ma was dead, and his da . . . But another thought crowded in on its heels. He had felt so safe, so happy these last couple months. Could something happen to ruin his new life, too?

Kip dragged a tired Nell into the Donaldson yard just as Dr. Donaldson was climbing into his buggy. "Hey, Kip, glad you're back. Got to go out to the Lesters'—horse got spooked and kicked out a fence. Got bad splinters festering the leg. Want to come?"

"Yes, *sir!*" Kip ignored Nell's pout as he hopped into the buggy and held on as Dr. Donaldson flicked his whip. The gray mare sprang into a fast trot.

Kip knew that Smack had been taken in by the Lesters, but he'd never been out to their place. Smack didn't like farm work and had run off once, showing up at the Donaldsons. But Kip had warned him he might get shipped back to New York, and then where would he be? Reluctantly, Smack had promised to give it another chance.

Mr. Lester met the buggy as the vet pulled into the farmyard. Smack stood a few feet away, looking

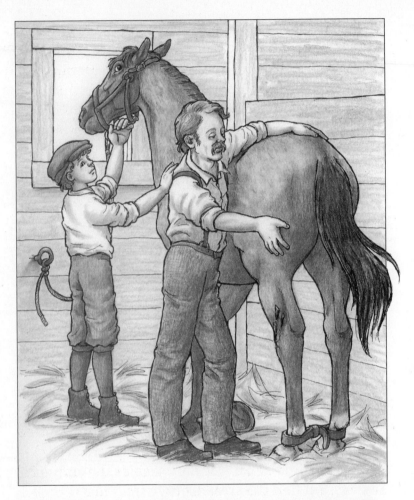

miserable. "Clumsy kid spooked my best horse." Mr. Lester glared at Kip like it was Kip's fault. But Dr. Donaldson said, "Come on, Kip. Need your help."

The horse was a tall, leggy roan, tied in a stall in the barn. It was favoring one hind leg and moving restlessly. "Don't know how you're going to dress it," Mr. Lester grumbled. "Won't let anyone near it."

Dr. Donaldson opened the stall and entered. "Whoa, boy, easy now . . ." His voice was soft and soothing. He laid a calm hand on the horse's back. The horse jerked his head up, trembling, but held still. The vet peered at the hind leg in the dim light of the barn. "Nasty splinters, all right. Lester, I need more light. Kip, get those hobbles from the buggy. Smack, get me a bucket of water."

Both boys were back in a few moments. Kip watched in admiration as Dr. Donaldson slipped the hobbles on before the horse even knew it. "Kip, get up by his head and keep talking to him, quiet like." Kip grabbed the roan's halter and murmured soothing words, keeping an eye on Dr. Donaldson as the vet ran a hand down the fevered leg, probed gently, then suddenly pulled. The horse jerked and almost fell down, but Dr. Donaldson gleefully held up a long, wicked splinter.

The process was repeated twice more, and finally Dr. Donaldson washed down the leg with a clean rag. He straightened. "That should do it." He bent to loosen the hobbles tied around the roan's fetlocks. Just at that moment, Mr. Lester said, "Let me see," and swung open the stall door with a bang.

The startled roan kicked out with its hind legs. With a yell, Dr. Donaldson fell backward, grabbing at his knee. Kip leaped to his side and pulled him out of range of the flailing horse. When they were clear, Mr. Lester slammed the stall door and latched it.

But the vet was crumpled on the barn floor, holding his right knee and moaning in pain.

Chapter 12

Home at Last

Somehow Mr. Lester, Smack, and Kip had gotten Dr. Donaldson into the buggy, and a frightened Kip had driven the gray mare home. *"Go get the doctor, Kip—hurry,"* Mrs. Donaldson had said, as she helped her moaning husband into the house.

Two weeks had passed. The leg wasn't broken but the tendons of the knee were badly torn. Dr. Donaldson still couldn't put any weight on his right leg. His wife made up a cot for him in the sitting room for the night, and during the day he had to keep his leg propped on a chair with two pillows. The bottle of pain medicine the doctor had left was almost gone.

When word got around that the vet was laid up for a while, the farmers had to call in a vet from another town when one of their animals got sick or injured. Kip did his best to keep up with the daily chores—keeping the woodbox filled, mucking out Misty's stall, and picking up milk at the nearest farm. But he could see that Dr. Donaldson was worried about the lost work and income.

Nell, however, took delight in her father's forced confinement and spent hours at his side cutting out paper dolls or working on her spelling. Tonight she was chatting away about the Christmas pageant practices that were going to start after school next week. "Mama came to school today, Papa, and assigned parts. Guess what! Peggy Conner is going to be Mary this year—Mama says she's perfect for the part. I'm going to be an angel; so is Carlotta, and Lena and Lauren—if they're still here, that is. Did you know their *real* mama wants to come take 'em back to New York?"

The hour was growing late and Kip still had evening chores to do. He took his jacket and cap off its peg and headed outside to check on the horse and close up the barn. Every time he thought about Lauren and Lena's mother showing up and wanting to take the girls away from the Stewarts, he got angry. Who was their *real* mother, anyway? Where was Mrs. Rogers when the governess dumped the girls at the Children's Aid Society? Where was she when Lena wouldn't talk or smile for months? What did Mrs. Rogers plan to do—take the girls back to New York, get another governess, and go skipping off to . . . to Spain or London or wherever the big passenger ships sailed to out of New York harbor?

As he pitched fresh hay into Misty's manger, Kip heard hoofbeats and the squeak of carriage wheels turn into the yard. Who was coming so late in the evening? Kip peeked out the door and saw the doctor's rig. But the doctor didn't stay long and was already gone by the time Kip dropped the bar on the barn doors and headed back to the house.

The kitchen was dark, but the lamp was still burning in the sitting room, and Kip could hear voices as he quietly opened the back door. Maybe he could slip silently up the stairs without—

Kip froze as he heard his name.

"—keep Kip any longer. Maybe we should write Rev. Brace."

"But, Ray! He's such a big help with all the heavy chores—*especially* now that you're laid up."

"But that's just it! Who knows how long I'll be laid up? How can we take on another mouth to feed—a hollow leg is more like it—and clothes and books and schooling, when I don't even know how I'm going to support my family."

"Oh, Ray." Mrs. Donaldson's voice seemed to wrap like warm arms around the discouraged tone of her husband. "The doctor said you could begin getting around if he ordered a brace for your knee—"

"Ha!" The sound was a cross between a laugh and a snort. "Order a brace indeed! Did you hear how much such a contraption costs? We don't have that kind of money—especially now."

Holding his breath, Kip took a candle from the hall and stole silently up the stairs to his little room under the eaves. He could still hear the low murmur of voices rising and falling below. He sat down on his bed and stared at the braided rug on the floor. Scraps of color went round and round in a spiral till it wound into a small knot in the middle. Like the knot in his stomach.

❖ ❖ ❖ ❖

It was after the Christmas pageant practice the following week when Kip decided what to do.

"Oh, Kip, we need a manger for the Baby Jesus," said Mrs. Donaldson at the first practice. "Do you think you could make something like that for us? It needs to be big enough to hold the Pattersons' baby."

Kip shrugged. "I guess so." But he was puzzled. A manger big enough to hold a baby? A manger was just a feed box for cows and horses. Babies were supposed to sleep in cradles. Like most of the former street rovers, Kip had never heard the Christmas story before, and didn't have a clue what sheep and shepherds and wise men and Baby Jesus had to do with each other. But they good-naturedly stood where Mrs. Donaldson placed them and said, "Behold! Glad tidings!" or "No room!" or "Look! A star!"

Kip was supposed to play Joseph, but Mrs. Donaldson had to keep reminding him of his lines. It was hard to concentrate. While Peggy (Mary, the mother of Jesus) and Davey (a sheep) and Hooter and Billy and Ned and Smack (shepherds and wise men) said their lines, Kip was wondering if Dr. Donaldson had written that letter to Rev. Brace.

Half the angels giggled constantly, but Kip noticed that the laughter in Lauren and Lena's eyes had been replaced by a troubled look . . . the same anxiety that knotted his own stomach and pushed against his brain.

Would he and Lauren and Lena be homeless again by Christmas?

It was already getting dark when Kip walked Nell home after practice. He quickly did his chores and began hunting for wood scraps to build the manger for the pageant. As he poked about the barn by lantern light, he found a broken barrel, old leather straps from a broken harness, a rusty wagon wheel, and boards from a former feed trough. Dumping all his findings in a pile, Kip ran back up to his room to get the leather cutter Mr. Rollins had given him when the shoemaking workshop folded. He could cut some strips from the old leather harness to lash the boards together . . . or he could whittle some pegs and fit the boards together like a nice box. . . .

Kip worked for several hours in the barn, stopping only briefly when Mrs. Donaldson called him in for supper. He was glad he had something to do that kept him out of the house, kept him from having to look Dr. Donaldson in the eyes. He was afraid he might beg: "Please! Let me stay!" But Kip was too proud to beg.

The manger wasn't hard to build, really, but as

Kip wrestled the metal rim from the broken barrel and neatly sliced some leather laces from the old harness, he looked with new interest at the metal and leather. He knew what leather and metal could do.

An idea began to form in his mind. All his life he had just let life happen to him—for good or bad. But he'd found something he wanted—wanted badly enough to fight for it. He wanted to stay with the Donaldsons. He wanted to work with the Doc. Someday he wanted to be a vet, just like Dr. Donaldson. He wanted a future!

No, he wouldn't beg. He had a better idea. He had to get the Doc up on his feet and back to work.

✧ ✧ ✧ ✧

Mrs. Donaldson said the manger was a fine piece of work—so sturdy! At least it wouldn't tip over and dump the Patterson baby out. That had happened last year, and Baby Jesus wailed so loudly, nobody could hear the wise men offer their gifts.

School was out and Christmas was only a week away when Lena took her pet rabbit to the Christmas pageant practice. She came over to Kip, rocking the rabbit from side to side in her arms. "If . . . if Lauren and me have to go back to . . . to New York . . ." A tear slid down the little girl's cheek. ". . . will you take care of Huffin for me?"

Kip felt trapped. He couldn't promise—*he* might be going back to New York himself. No! . . . He couldn't think like that. And he couldn't let Lena think like that, either.

"Hey. Huffin doesn't want ta hear ya talkin' 'bout leavin' him." Kip was tempted to laugh. Muffin, Puffin, Huffin . . . where did Lena think up these names? "I think what Huffin wants is ta be in the pageant; what ya say? Davey's a sheep—he can look after him while the angels sing. Now, go along with ya—I'll talk to Mrs. Donaldson."

Lauren had told Kip another letter had come from Rev. Brace. Mrs. Rogers wanted to see the girls, but was willing to talk about where the best place was for them. Rev. Brace said he would accompany her to Dowagiac sometime before the first of the year so the Stewarts and Mrs. Rogers could sit down together.

So. Rev. Brace was coming. Was he coming to pick up Kip, as well?

Kip spent every spare minute out in the barn experimenting with the leather and pieces of metal he had found. Knowing that Rev. Brace was coming, Kip had a sudden pang of guilt. Would he say Kip was stealing these items from the Donaldsons? Oh, wouldn't the judge like to be proved right! A quick trip to the kitchen, asking permission from Mrs. Donaldson to use the broken items he'd found, set his mind at ease.

Dress rehearsal for the Christmas pageant was the night before Christmas Eve. Kip could hardly keep his mind on his lines. "Come, Mary, we must go ta Bethlehem ta be taxed." . . . "I'm sorry, Mary, a stable is all I could find." Mrs. Donaldson had to prompt him several times because his mind was on whether his idea was going to work. Tonight he would find out.

After all the other children had left, Kip and Nell helped Mrs. Donaldson set all the props in place for the pageant the next night. They locked the church-schoolhouse door and walked quickly home, hunched against the cold. "Oh, I wish Daddy could come to the pageant!" Nell cried, blowing out puffs of white air. "Can he, Mama? Can he—oh, look! It's snowing!" The little girl skipped ahead excitedly.

Kip shivered. Snow in New York just meant misery for man and beast alike.

Dr. Donaldson was dozing in the sitting room when the trio arrived. "Did you try walking around with that cane like the doctor told you?" asked Mrs. Donaldson, pulling off her gloves.

Her husband sighed. "I did try. But every time I bend that knee . . . I don't know." Discouragement hung heavy on his face.

Kip slipped out the back door and ran to the barn. In a few minutes he was back, holding a strange contraption that looked something like a stiff horse halter. "Uh . . . Dr. Donaldson? I made somethin' fer ya . . . a Christmas present like. It . . . it don't look like much, but . . . well, I won't know if it's gonna work 'less I try it on ya."

Dr. Donaldson looked at his wife, but she looked just as puzzled as he did.

"It's a knee brace, Doc . . . metal on the sides an'

around the top an' bottom, covered with leather pieces stitched front and back. Might keep ya knee straight till it gets strong again. Now . . . will ya try it on?"

Dr. Donaldson stuck out his injured leg. "Got nothing to lose, have we? Go on . . . put it on."

Kip knelt down and slid the brace up Dr. Donaldson's right leg till it fit over his knee. Then he pulled the stiff pieces together with finely cut leather laces and tied them tightly.

Mrs. Donaldson helped her husband stand up. He took the cane she handed him and walked slowly across the room, his right leg stiff. He turned and started back, gaining confidence with each step. "This thing just might work," he murmured. "It really supports my knee!" He turned to Kip. "*You* made this, Kip? Just thought it up? Figured it out yourself?" He turned and started back across the room. "Amazing," he muttered. "Just amazing!"

❖ ❖ ❖

The next night the church-schoolhouse was packed. Snow had been falling off and on since the night before, but it didn't keep anyone home. All the townsfolk and farming families came to see their children participate in the yearly Christmas pageant.

The excited children kept peeking out from behind the sheet strung across the front of the room. "Did ya see my folks out there?" Smack grinned at

Kip. Smack's shepherd headdress kept slipping off to one side, giving him a comical one-eyed-bandit look. "Mr. Lester ain't said nothin' more about *me* spookin' the horse. Been treatin' me more civil-like, too."

"Shh, children." Mrs. Donaldson ushered the last stray sheep and wise man behind the sheet. "We're about to begin."

From behind the sheet, Kip could hear the little pump organ wheeze as the people began to sing "O Come, All Ye Faithful," followed by "The First Noel." Then Lauren stepped out from behind the sheet to begin her narration:

" 'And it came to pass in those days, that there went out a decree from Caesar Augustus, that all the world should be taxed. And all went to be taxed, every one into his own city.' "

That was Kip's cue. He took Peggy's arm and pushed the sheet aside. "Come, Mary, we must go ta Bethlehem ta be taxed."

As "Joseph" and "Mary" slowly walked around the perimeter of the schoolhouse, Kip had a strange feeling. Long ago, the real Joseph and Mary had gone on a long, difficult journey, just like he and Peggy and the others on the orphan train. And when they got to the strange town, they didn't know if they'd find a place to stay.

"No room!" said Hooter, the innkeeper.

Kip's cue. "I'm sorry, Mary, a stable is all I could find."

The pump organ wheezed out "Silent Night" as the manger was brought out and Peggy went to get the Patterson baby. Kip stood by her stool as "Mary" rocked "Baby Jesus." The baby smiled up at her. Kip had that funny feeling again. *Baby Jesus knew what it was like to be homeless, too. But God took care of His Son anyway, because He had an important future.*

Kip was so lost in these new thoughts that he almost didn't notice the door of the schoolhouse open and two figures—a man and a woman—slip in. But Smack the shepherd poked him in the ribs and whispered, "Hey. Rev. Brace just come in . . . an' some woman. Do ya think it's Lauren and Lena's real ma?"

The newcomers were sitting in the back and Kip couldn't see. But his heart sank. If Rev. Brace and Mrs. Rogers were here, this might be *his* last night in Dowagiac, too.

A gentle laugh swept the audience as Davey the sheep scooted in and held up Huffin the white rabbit to see the Baby Jesus. The grinning wise men placed their gifts beside the manger, and the little organ pumped out the final song, "Joy to the World!"

The pageant was over.

Kip saw Rev. Brace start to push his way toward the front. Kip quickly looked around for Lauren and Lena. He didn't have to look far. Lena, still wearing her white angel smock, had snatched up Huffin and run to Mrs. Stewart, hiding her face in her foster mother's lap.

"Kip O'Reilly! Peggy Conner!" Rev. Brace's voice was as big as his smile. "A wonderful performance! I'm so glad we got here in time to see some of it."

The woman behind him peeked around Rev. Brace's shoulder, her eyes twinkling and cheeks dimpling. Kip's mouth dropped open. The woman with Rev. Brace was *Mrs.* Brace!

"But . . . but I thought . . . I mean, we thought . . ."

Rev. Brace's eyebrows went up. "What? Oh! You thought Mrs. Rogers was coming with me! Of course you did . . . where are the Stewarts? And Lauren and Lena. No need to say this twice."

Mr. and Mrs. Stewart came forward with Lauren and Lena clinging tightly to their hands. "Well," said Rev. Brace, "a slight change in plans. At the last minute, Mrs. Rogers—the girls' mother—was summoned back to Europe by her husband to settle some business affairs. She admitted that with all the traveling she does, the girls are no doubt better off here with the Stewarts, after all. But . . ." Rev. Brace leaned down to look into Lauren's and Lena's eyes. "She wants to come see you, and she will write. All in good time."

He straightened. "But since I already had two train tickets . . . and since I also had a letter from Dr. Donaldson that needed attention, Letitia decided to come with me—and here we are!"

Kip's throat tightened. So Dr. Donaldson had written Rev. Brace, after all.

"I'm sorry, then, that you wasted a trip." Dr. Donaldson limped up to the small group at the front of the schoolhouse. Mrs. Donaldson waved good-bye to some of the children and joined them. The vet laid a hand on Kip's shoulder. "I wrote that letter when I was feeling desperate—not sure how I was going to support my family, much less an adopted son. But I've changed my mind."

An adopted son? Changed his mind? Kip felt confused. What was happening here?

Mrs. Donaldson chimed in. "What Ray's trying to say, Rev. Brace, is that we'd like to adopt Kip as our son. We're not sure how we ever got along without him! In fact, Ray is here tonight because Kip gave him a priceless gift—the ability to get back on his feet."

Kip was astonished. Not just stay, but . . . adopted?

She turned to Kip. "We were going to tell you tomorrow—for Christmas."

Dr. Donaldson nodded. "This is one clever boy, Rev. Brace. He's going to go far. But it's not just because he invented this knee brace for me. My wife and I had already decided we wanted Kip to become part of our family—no matter what."

Nell squealed and jumped up and down. "Now I've got my very own big brother!"

"Not just yours," stormed a childish voice. Davey Conner squeezed into the little group. "Kip promised he'd always be my big brother."

"He's my big brother, too . . . kinda," said Lena, rocking Huffin back and forth. "He whittled me a toy rabbit when I lost Muffin."

The adults laughed. "I think," said Rev. Brace, "that the children from the orphan train have a thing or two to teach all of us about being God's family."

When the last lamp was finally blown out, the last good-byes said, Kip stood on the steps of the church-schoolhouse and looked around the town of Dowagiac, slowly being buried under the softly falling snow.

He was home at last.

More About Charles Loring Brace

Charles Loring Brace was born in Litchfield, Connecticut, June 19, 1826. He was educated for the clergy and ordained as a Methodist minister. But at the age of twenty-six he was asked to head up the newly forming Children's Aid Society of New York, which became his life ministry. A true humanitarian, Rev. Brace walked the streets of New York that were swollen with successive tides of immigrants. He talked with people from all walks of life until he knew all its infrastructures and human predicaments. His focus became the neglected "street children" and other children of poverty. Here he felt there was hope for redeeming their young lives, their fate not yet hardened. An astute social analyst as well, Brace believed addressing the needs of these thousands of street children was mandatory if society hoped to prevent a growing "dangerous class" of criminals sucking on society just to survive.

But Brace was against "charity" for its own sake. He believed that orphanages (and institutional life in general), and even "soup kitchens" that simply handed out meals, developed an unhealthy dependence on "being done for" rather than "doing for oneself." All Brace's efforts—newsboy lodging houses, Sunday boys' meetings, industrial schools, night schools, and workshops—were efforts to help the young help themselves.

But even these efforts fell short, as far as Rev. Brace was concerned. True reformation of a young life could only take place in a family setting, preferably in the country or small town, in which a young person could experience a normal life at its best. To Brace, the best possibility for addressing the "dangerous classes" was to remove homeless children from New York and send them to "good Christian homes" in the West. This was mutually beneficial, because farm families could always use additional helping hands. The children, however, were not to be "indentured servants" or "apprentices," but taken into the family as foster children with all the rights and privileges (as well as responsibilities) of natural children. Some children were even adopted.

At this time in history, with westward expansion and the building of the railroads across the country, the primary mode of transporting children to the Midwest was by train. Thus, the "orphan trains" were born, a systematic "placing out" of children that continued for almost seventy-five years. Though the plan had its critics and occasional failures, about two hundred thousand children were placed in families, most of whom grew up to become productive citizens. The Society made every attempt to follow up on the children they placed, and a report in 1910 said that eighty-seven percent were "doing well."

Charles Loring Brace was a prolific writer—of letters, pamphlets, articles, and books—and a tireless speaker on behalf of neglected children. His persuasive arguments won support from "the better classes" for his humanitarian efforts.

He married Miss Letitia Neill in Belfast, Ireland, on August 21, 1854, returning to New York and the fledgling Children's Aid Society in September. Mrs. Brace was a great support to her husband's humanitarian efforts, not the least of which was providing an oasis of sanity and civility in their homelife, a refuge from the dreadful conditions he encountered daily in his work with street children.

Though committed to his work in the city, Rev. Brace drew great inspiration and renewal from the country. He decided that city children could benefit from exposure to the country, as well. In 1875, a summer home was established where street children could spend a week in the fresh air by the sea. Later, after his death, the Brace Memorial Farm was established where street children could not only learn farming skills, but manners and personal social skills to help prepare them for family life.

Charles Loring Brace died of Bright's disease on August 11, 1890, but his son, C. L. Brace, Jr., and other dedicated agents continued his work. The orphan trains finally came to an end in the 1920s, as changing social attitudes about family focused on keeping families together, and changing laws helped curb child labor and established compulsory education.

But in the latter part of the nineteenth century, Charles Loring Brace and the Children's Aid Society of New York had worked tirelessly to save the lives of thousands of neglected children, most of whom became productive citizens and include: a governor of a state, a governor of a territory, members of Congress, district attorneys, sheriffs, mayors, judges, college professors, clergymen, school principals, teachers, artists, railroad officials, journalists, bankers, physicians, lawyers, civil engineers, businessmen, mechanics, farmers, and servicemen and women, as well as husbands and wives and parents.

For Further Reading

Brace, Charles Loring. *The Dangerous Classes of New York and Twenty Years' Work Among Them.* Montclair, New Jersey: Patterson Smith, 1967 (reprint).

Brace, Emma, ed. *The Life of Charles Loring Brace: Chiefly Told in His Own Letters.* London: Sampson Low, Marston, & Co., Ltd., 1894 © by Charles Scribner's Sons for the United States of America.

Fry, Annette R. *The Orphan Trains*. New York: New Discovery Books, Macmillan Publishing Company, 1994.

Patrick, Michael; Sheets, Evelyn; and Trickel, Evelyn. *We Are a Part of History: The Story of the Orphan Trains*. Virginia Beach: The Donning Company/Publishers, 1990.

Patrick, Michael and Trickel, Evelyn. *Orphan Trains to Missouri*. Columbia, Missouri: University of Missouri Press, 1997.

Warren, Andrea. *Orphan Train Rider: One Boy's True Story*. Boston: Houghton Mifflin Company, 1996.

For more exciting stories from Dave and Neta Jackson, read any of their four *Hero Tales* collections. Here's an excerpt from *Volume IV*:

JOHN HARPER

The *Titanic's* Last Hero

Born to a Scottish family on May 29, 1872, in the village of Houston in Renfrewshire, John Harper grew up surrounded by a solid Christian faith. As a lad, he faithfully attended church, was not rebellious or wild, and at the age of fourteen, gave his life to the Lord. But like many boys of his time, he was eager to prove his manhood by getting a job; while still in his teens he went to work in the local paper mill.

But in 1890, just after his eighteenth birthday, he was home alone on a fine June day and had what he called a vision from God. God showed him that "good" people and "wicked" people are both lost without Christ, and that Christ's death on the cross was the *only* thing that had saved him. He was overwhelmed by God's great love, and a passion began to grow within him to share God's love and win "the lost" for Christ. After a long workday in the paper mill, he would go to the surrounding villages and preach on the street corners.

In 1896 an English pastor from a Baptist mission in London heard about the young street-corner evangelist and invited him to become part of their mission in Govan, a "burgh" of Glasgow, Scotland. After a year and a half, he was sent to Gordon Halls on Paisley Road (near Glasgow) and started the Paisley Road Baptist Church with twenty-five members. A few years later, a church building was erected nearby out of corrugated iron, which came to be nicknamed "the Iron Church."

John Harper not only had the zeal of an evangelist, but a pastor's heart. Within thirteen years, Paisley Road Baptist Church had grown to five hundred people. But during this time he was severely tested. In 1904 he married Annie Bell, who brought great joy to his life, but that joy was short-lived. Two years later she gave birth to a daughter but died shortly afterward, leaving behind a motherless infant. A year earlier (1905), John had been seriously ill for six months, which left both his body and powerful voice weakened.

But John Harper's faith was in God, and he still wanted to share the Gospel. In September 1910, he left the thriving Paisley Road church to become pastor of the Walworth Road Baptist Church in London. News of his powerful preaching and the many people who were being saved under his ministry spread, and he was invited by Moody Church in Chicago to conduct "special services" in the winter of 1911–1912. The special services became a revival, and he was invited to return to Chicago in April 1912. Harper booked passage for himself and six-year-old Nana on the *Lusitania*, but for reasons unknown changed his ticket to the *Titanic*, which sailed from London on April 10.

John Harper never arrived in Chicago. Little Nana was saved when the "unsinkable ship" sank five nights later, but John Harper went down with the ship. His actions that fateful night can only be described as heroic. He was thirty-nine years old, still a young man, but in both heavenly and earthly terms, he can well be called "the *Titanic*'s last hero."

ZEAL

Crowning King Jesus

~~~~~~

Paul Morris[2] put on his cap, stuck the day's newspaper under his arm, and walked jauntily to his girl's house on the outskirts of Glasgow, Scotland. "Would've been grand to be in London today." He grinned as the young couple settled on a bench in her mother's garden. Paul opened up the paper and jabbed a thick finger at the headlines under the date—August 9, 1902. "Just imagine all that pomp and ceremony when they crowned King Edward!"

"Aye, that'd sure be a sight," murmured Glynis, but she seemed distracted. "Don'na know what to do about tomorrow, though."

"Tomorrow?" said her suitor absently, his mind still on the king's coronation.

Glynis sighed. "Some church workers came by the house last night—they got a promise from Mama that we'd come to the church services over on Paisley Road tomorrow night."

Paul snorted. "Is that the church that's been holding out-door services all summer? Lots of preachin' and hallelujahs and loud amens?"

Glynis giggled. "That's the one. Come with me. Just for a lark."

---

[2]Note: We do not know this person's name, only his initials: P. C. M.

"Humph. Can think of a lot of things I'd rather do with my Sunday evening," he mumbled.

But Sunday evening, August 10, found a reluctant Paul escorting his girl into the Paisley Road Baptist Church. Two deacons shook their hands warmly and showed them to a seat. As the service began, an open hymnbook was put into their hands. The singing was hearty—a definite improvement, Paul thought, over the sleepy drone that passed for hymn singing at his own church. But then a tall, slender man—John Harper, the pastor of Paisley Road Baptist Church—announced the sermon text: Isaiah 44:20. The pastor's voice was powerful as he read the Scripture: " 'He feedeth on ashes. . . .' "

Paul Morris couldn't remember exactly what the pastor said—only that John Harper's words cut like a knife into his soul. Paul realized that "religion" by itself was like eating ashes. Going to church couldn't save him. Only Jesus Christ could do that. At the end of the service, Pastor Harper asked all those who wanted to trust Christ as Savior to raise their hand. Paul Morris's hand shot up. And in that moment he realized an important transfer had taken place: He got off the throne of his life and crowned Jesus king.

After church, one of the members stopped to talk to Paul and his sweetheart. "Are you trusting Jesus?" the man asked Glynis.

She shrugged but replied honestly, "No."

"What about you, young man?"

Paul squared his shoulders. "Yes."

Glynis's eyes widened. "That's not true!" she cried. "You didn't even want to come tonight."

But the church member persisted. "How long have you known Christ as Savior?"

"Since Pastor Harper gave the invitation just a few minutes ago." Turning to Glynis, Paul said, "It's true, I didn't want to come. But Pastor Harper's sermon convinced me that I need Jesus. I asked Him to come into my life and save me."

To Paul's surprise, Glynis began to weep, and within a few minutes she, too, asked Jesus to be her Savior.

As the young couple, soon to be married, walked away from Paisley Road Baptist Church, they passed an old man and heard the church member ask him, "Are you trusting in Jesus?"

"Oh yes," said the old man. "Nine years now."

"How old were you then?"

"Just turned seventy."

"And how did it come about?"

Curious, Paul and Glynis turned to hear the last bit of conversation with the old man. White-haired and bent, he still had a wide smile. "Nine years ago there was no church here. But that young man—that Mr. Harper—he was out on a street corner preaching Jesus, and I trusted Him as Savior there and then."

Zeal is doing something for God
with everything you've got.

FROM GOD'S WORD:

Love the Lord your God with all your heart, all your soul, all your mind, and all your strength (Mark 12:30).

LET'S TALK ABOUT IT:

1. From this story, what do you think Pastor John Harper wanted to do more than anything?
2. How do you know he was willing to give it "everything he got"?
3. What are some ways you can love God with *all* your heart? *All* your soul? *All* your mind? *All* your strength?

SELF-SACRIFICE

"It Will Be Beautiful in the Morning"

~~~~~~

John Harper held little Nana's hand tightly as they walked the deck of the big ship. He smiled at the child fondly, thinking how much she looked like the mother she had never known.

"Papa, this ship is so *big*!" Nana said as they rounded the bow and started back down the other side of the *Titanic*. "It's as big as a whole city!"

John chuckled and was about to agree, when he noticed a young man hunched beside the deck rail. "Just a minute, darling . . . this young man looks like he needs to hear the Good News."

Nana peeked through the rails and patiently watched the sun settling down on the edge of the water as she listened to the familiar sound of her father explaining how to be saved. After a while the young man turned and walked away. Nana once again put her hand in her father's and pointed at the horizon. "Look, Papa—the sky is so red!"

"Yes, I see, darling. 'Red sky at night, sailors delight . . .' It's going to be beautiful in the morning."

It was late. Nana should be in bed. John Harper took his little girl and tucked her into her bunk in their cabin, then settled down at the tiny desk to read by lamplight before going to bed himself.

Shortly before midnight the ship seemed to shudder. Not

long afterward, urgent voices were heard in the narrow hall-way. "Everybody out! Everybody out!" John pulled on his clothes, bundled Nana into her cloak, and went up on deck. Panic spread the word: An iceberg had grazed the ship, tearing open a gaping hole, and the ship was taking on water.

Life jackets were handed out. People started pushing and scrambling to get into the lifeboats. "Let the women, children, and the unsaved into the lifeboats!" John shouted. He swung little Nana into a lifeboat, then turned back to help others as flares shot into the sky.

John spotted a man without a life jacket. "Are you saved, brother?" he asked. The man looked at him angrily and tried to brush him aside. "Here," said John, taking off his life jacket. "You need this more than I do."

As the dark, cold waters of the North Atlantic crept up the decks of the *Titanic*, John Harper's calm, reasoning voice could be heard helping to load people into the lifeboats, and asking first one, then another and another, "Brother . . . sister, are you saved? It's not too late! Ask God to forgive your sins and accept Jesus as your Lord and Savior. Be sure where you will spend eternity!"

At 2:20 A.M., the stern of the giant ship rose in the air, and the *Titanic* began its long plunge to the bottom of the ocean. John Harper was thrown into the icy water. All around him were the desperate cries of drowning men and women. A man clinging to a board drifted near the floundering Harper. "Are you saved?" Harper shouted.

"No," the man gasped.

"Believe on the Lord Jesus Christ, and thou shall be saved," John Harper shouted back.

The icy waters were taking their toll. John Harper's strength was giving out. He saw the man float back within call-ing distance. "Are you saved?" he shouted again.

"No," came the weak reply.

"Then believe on the Lord Jesus Christ, and thou shall be

saved," he urged before slipping beneath the water.

The man clinging to the board was later picked up by a rescue ship. John Harper's last words burned in his mind, and he gave his heart to Christ. He was John Harper's last convert.

As the sun rose on the scene of the disaster on April 15, 1912, it *was* a beautiful morning—but for John Harper, that morning was in heaven, where he met the Savior he loved so much, face-to-face.

࿐

Self-sacrifice is loving as Jesus loved—a willingness
to give up my life so that others might live.

FROM GOD'S WORD:

This is my command: Love each other as I have loved you. The greatest love a person can show is to die for his friends (John 15:12–13, NCV).

LET'S TALK ABOUT IT:

1. Why do you think John Harper didn't get into the lifeboat with Nana, even though he knew she would become an orphan?
2. Everybody on the *Titanic* wanted to be "saved" from drowning. But when John Harper asked, "Are you saved?" what did he mean?
3. Are *you* saved?